P9-APH-807

JASMIN

JASMIN

Jan Truss

A Groundwood Book
Douglas & McIntyre
Vancouver

Copyright © 1982 by Jan Truss
Third printing, 1990

All rights reserved. No part of this book may be reproduced or transmitted in any
form by any means without permission in writing from the publisher, except by a
reviewer, who may quote brief passages in a review.

Douglas & McIntyre Limited,
1615 Venables Street
Vancouver, British Columbia.

Canadian Cataloguing in Publication Data
Truss, Jan.
  Jasmin

ISBN 0-88899-014-6 (pbk.)

I. Title.

PS8589.R87J37   jC813'.54   C82-094031-3
PZ7.T78Ja

Published in the United States of America as a
Margaret K. McElderry Book by Atheneum

Cover illustration by Margaret Farrell Bruno

Printed and bound in Canada by D. W. Friesen & Sons Ltd.

For a boy called Jim,
who did not find the golden house
in the forest,
and
For Fraser Jon,
who lives in a golden house.

MEG MERRILIES

by John Keats, circa 1815

Old Meg she was a gipsy
   And lived upon the moors:
Her bed it was the brown heath turf,
   Her house was out of doors.

Her apples were swart blackberries,
   Her currants pods o'broom;
Her wine was dew of the wild white rose,
   Her book a churchyard tomb.

Her brothers were the craggy hills,
   Her sisters larchen trees—
Alone with her great family
   She lived as she did please.

No breakfast had she many a morn,
   No dinner many a noon,
And 'stead of supper she would stare
   Full hard against the moon.

But, every morn, of woodbine fresh
   She made her garlanding,
And every night the dark glen yew
   She wove, and she would sing.

And with her fingers old and brown,
   She plaited mats o'rushes
And gave them to the cottagers
   She met among the bushes.

Old Meg was brave as Margaret Queen,
   And tall as Amazon:
An old red blanket cloak she wore;
   A chip hat had she on.
God rest her aged bones somewhere—
   She died full long agone!

JASMIN

1

THE SEVEN STALKE CHILDREN WERE IN THEIR BEDS in the steep-sided attic of their log home. Six of the children were sleeping. The seventh, Jasmin Marie Antoinette, lay awake watching the bright moon through the high, bare window. Her bed was in the best place—under the window—because she was the oldest. She was watching the moon sail through the tall treetops because she could not sleep for worrying. That night she knew for certain sure she was going to fail the sixth grade.

How could she live if she didn't pass into grade seven? How could she live if she had to stay in the elementary school while all the other kids from her class went off to the junior high school in Witchitt, a town to the east, where the wooded hills had already changed into flat prairie fields and a wide highway went south to the big rodeo city of Calgary?

How could Jasmin Marie Antoinette Stalke stand being left to cope with a new bunch of kids who would all laugh at her silly fancy name? Her big fat jolly mother was romantic about babies—she didn't seem to care about the population explosion —and she found glamorous names for each new one. The baby, who at that very moment was howling in the room underneath, was called Honey Angelina—

which might be all right for a sticky baby. But, just wait till she got to school! What if she turned out to be a spoiled brat with a face like a witch and with a name like that?

Jasmin Marie Antoinette Stalke was embarrassed by every bit of her name. Her mother said it was for a queen. Some queen! Jasmin knew she was plain—thin, with ordinary blue eyes and ordinary straight brown hair that hung long to her waist. Nobody had ever taken the trouble to tell her eyes were as blue as deep mountain lakes and her hair thick and shiny like the coat of a mountain lion. Instead, people were always telling her to "take that insolent look off your face." No doubt that was because she often stuck out her chin to pretend she didn't care about a lot of things.

But she did care. That night she lay in bed, in angry despair, going over all the bad things in her life. She wasn't pretty. Her hair was straight. She was flat-chested. Now her grandmother was dead she didn't get any pretty clothes. All the boys thought she was an ugly dummy. Nobody liked her. She wasn't good at sports. She wasn't good at anything.

She decided there was no use in trying anymore.

The worst trouble of all was that her teachers gave too much homework. How could she do homework properly with so many little brothers and sisters yelling, climbing over everything, quarrelling and messing things up? That very day she had failed the social studies test because Leroy Lorne Raphael, her retarded brother, the one nearest in age to her, had thrown her school workbook down the hole in the smelly outhouse.

She didn't mind the outhouse most of the time. When she used the flush toilets at school, there were only bare walls and the feet in the next cubicle to look at, but the old outhouse was lined with ancient newspapers to keep out drafts. And sometimes, when she rushed out there in the early morning, the pathway through the trees was hung with dew-sprinkled spiders' webs. Often she'd leave the door open a little bit so she could watch the squirrels running on invisible pathways through the high pine branches. Blue jays flashed and glided. Sometimes the whole outside morning sang with birds. Oh, but on cold winter nights, the outhouse could be terrible. Then she would dash quickly back into the hot, teeming house.

The Stalke house was in the dense bush, on the edge of civilisation in western Canada. It was west of the village of Dandron where Jasmin went to the twelve-room elementary school. The kids, who went home westwards from Dandron on the school bus, sometimes lost their stomachs on the steep downhills, and from the hilltops they looked across massive valleys of forests that reached to the Rocky Mountains where snow always glimmered.

From the road the Stalke house was plain to see, an old thing behind a junkyard of overturned cars and rusted farm machinery. The house itself wasn't so bad. It was a log house that had been built ages ago by pioneers to be the first school in the district. It was the junkyard that was so terrible. It was one of the things Jasmin stuck her chin out about to pretend she didn't care.

The real trouble with the inside of the house was that there were only two rooms besides the attic, where the children slept. The big one, long ago, had held desks for twenty children and one for the teacher, a woodstove, a piano, cupboards and bookshelves. The smaller one had been a cloakroom. Now it was her parents' bedroom and on one of its walls there were still the curly iron hooks that those pioneer children had hung their coats on. Once a teacher had gushed to Jasmin, "How very romantic it must be to live in a real pioneer home." How romantic! That's what she thought. She doesn't have to live here, Jasmin thought now, as she lay sleepless, watching the moon.

The big room was the *for everything room*. Both cooking and eating were done there. That's where everyone took a bath once a week in a long tin tub for everybody to see. All the kids played there, watched TV and tried to do homework. The TV was never switched off. Jasmin was getting to hate that *for everything room,* blaming it when she couldn't get her homework done. It was easy for girls who had nice bedrooms to themselves and somewhere to be quiet with their own things, to do their studying.

She watched the moon and thought *hate, hate, hate*. No private place. Nothing to call her own. Nothing except one thing. Her mood brightened a little bit as she thought of the secret cupboard under the roof just behind her bed.

6

In pioneer days the attic had been the teacher's bedroom, and in that small cupboard there were still some faded, long-ago teacher's books. Most kids would think she was crazy for counting a dingy cupboard and some old books as a precious secret. Jasmin knew that, and so she would never tell anybody and risk being laughed at.

One book was most special to her. It was small and thin, soft to feel. It was covered in brown leather and the edges of its pages were still gold. She felt sure it had once been somebody else's long-ago treasure. On the inside cover, in spiky, sloping, faded brown handwriting it simply said, *For Meg, 1894*.

Often, Jasmin wondered who Meg had been. One thing was certain—she was lucky to have had such a simple name. And she was lucky to have had somebody to give her the book, *Favorite Poems for Children*. Anybody could tell that those old-fashioned poems wouldn't be favorites for kids now, but Jasmin liked them. She didn't know what a lot of the words meant, but somehow, the book and the poems gave her a good feeling. What was wrong with that?

But the kids at school would laugh at her if they knew about her inside feelings. Especially they would laugh if they found out she liked poems. That was another thing to stick her chin out about.

Now, to make herself less depressed, she stood up in the silver moonlight, reached up above the iron bedrail and stealthily took the little book from its dark cupboard, her fingers recognising it by its softness. Leroy stirred in his sleep and shouted strange words from his dreams. She held her breath and stood very still, staring hard at Leroy's big head and white hair, by her stillness willing him to calm down. His white eyelashes fluttered as he muttered broken sounds. Downstairs her father was watching the late movie. Roars and blasts of TV sound pushed up through the floorboards with shouting and guns and police sirens. The Honey Angelina baby was still howling. Jasmin looked away from Leroy to the faraway moon so silently passing. She felt hopeless.

She couldn't go to school tomorrow. No way! She couldn't face all the kids knowing she was definitely going to fail. It was bad enough that she had failed the social studies test. On that test she hadn't been able to name any of the places on the map where cars are manufactured near Toronto. She hadn't been able to name places where uranium and asbestos are mined. All the information she had needed to study had been in that workbook down the hole in the smelly outhouse. Then, as though that wasn't enough, her science project had been ruined.

She was counting on her science project to prove she could stick at an assignment and do something well. The science project was more important than a regular assignment. It was work to be displayed at the big Science Fair held every year in the Witchitt Community Arena. Everybody in all the communities for miles around talked about the projects for weeks afterwards, everybody except

Jasmin's family. They didn't really care about things like that.

My parents don't understand, Jasmin thought hopelessly.

It was as though they lived in a different time in history, as though they had got left behind in pioneer times. Bud Stalke still struggled with antique farm machinery that was always breaking down. He dressed like a TV cowboy with pointy boots, tight jeans, and a high-crowned cowboy hat. Her mother was like a pioneer woman, giving her breast to so many babies. The boys at school were always making dirty jokes about the "Storky" family, making Jasmin stick out her chin to hide her embarrassment.

She had worked very hard at that science project. She wanted to show the different growth rates of two sweet potatoes when one was grown in the gray soil from under the pine trees and the other in black loam from a prairie field. She had lettered neat signs to explain what she was doing, keeping exact charts of the first root, the first shoot, the first leaf, the daily, carefully-measured growth of each of her two plants.

It had been lovely having the growing plants on the window ledge above her bed, especially when the tendrils stretched out and spread leaves across the window. For safety from all the little brothers and sisters she had kept her signs and charts up there on the high ledge, out of reach.

But that morning, one of the impish brothers,

Nathaniel Augustus John, had stomachache so badly he had been left in the outhouse when the school bus came. So he had stayed home all day looking for mischief. He had merry blue eyes, black curly hair, and was chubby like a Valentine card angel. Some angel! During the day he persuaded Leroy to be Tarzan and swing out through the attic window on a rope knotted onto the iron post of Jasmin's bed. Poor trusting Leroy, he had swung out like Tarzan in the jungle—and all of Jasmin's science project had swung out with him.

She had arrived home from school, depressed by the terrible social-studies test, to find her mother's bright bantam hens clucking and scratching all over her beautiful signs and charts where they had fallen among the overturned cars and junk machinery. She wanted to scream and cry. Instead she hardened her eyes and stuck her chin out.

Her plants, with all their soil, had been flung out of their orange and green plastic ice-cream buckets; then they had been broken and trampled by her mother fussing over bruised and frightened Leroy.

Jasmin bit her lip when she looked at the poor dead things, the leaves blackened, the graceful stems twisted and flattened. So—Jasmin Marie Antoinette Stalke would be the only student who didn't have a science project. That was the end!

When she started to complain her mother just patted her on the back and said cheerfully, "Now smarten up Jasmin, willya? I've got more important things to worry about than your potted plants. Come on, be a good girl. Go and pump me up a bucket of nice fresh water."

Well, it wasn't any good crying. So Jasmin hauled in water, helped make supper, got the little kids to bed. She didn't bother to do any homework. It wasn't worth it. She just didn't see how she could go to school ever again. The only one without a science project. The only one *failing*.

The moon disappeared behind a dark cloud. The long attic went very black. Leroy cried out. The little kids' breathing sounded like snakes sliding and rustling.

Jasmin held her breath and put her precious book against her cheek. In the dark moment, she suddenly knew what she had to do. Words from the book came very clearly into her head, clear as a spoken message:

> *Old Meg she was a gipsy*
> *And lived upon the moors;*
> *Her bed it was the brown heath turf,*
> *Her house was out of doors.*

The book was showing her a way out, telling her she must leave the house and her problems. It was telling her to run away and live like Meg in the poem.

> *Her brothers were the craggy hills*
> *Her sisters larchen trees*
> *Alone with her great family*
> *She lived as she did please.*

11

Oh, what a dream to live *as she did please*.

It would be easy to run away and live in the outdoors, to live in the thick shelter of the forests on the edge of the Rocky Mountains.

When the moon came out from behind the cloud, silvering the beds and the sleeping children again, Jasmin had made up her mind. As soon as the TV was switched off and the baby settled, she would slip out into the moonlight to run away under the lovely early summer stars.

Jasmin Marie Antoinette Stalke, like the Meg in her favorite poem, would make her bed on the brown heath turf and she would *live as she did please*.

2

AT LAST THE HOUSE WAS QUIET. BY THAT TIME JASMIN was already dressed. She had found her clothes by moonlight. Her underwear was warm from being under her pillow, her jeans and T-shirt cool and crumpled from the floorboards. She rolled up her patchwork quilt, the one her grandmother had made especially for her before she died. It was stuffed lightly with goose feathers and made from bright bits of cloth from grandmother's marvelous rag bag. "A girl deserves a pretty thing," her grandmother had often said when Jasmin was still little. Then grandmother had grown ill so that her clever fingers only worked slowly and with difficulty. The bright patchwork quilt was the last thing she made. Jasmin rolled it up small and tied it round with the rope Leroy and Nathaniel had used for playing Tarzan. It was good luck they had left it tied to her bed. She made two loops in it so she could carry the quilt on her back, like a backpack.

She dragged out her puffy, dark-green winter parka from under her bed trying not to make a sound. Then she tucked the soft little leather book in the pocket in the lining of the parka. Not a real pocket, but a sort of secret opening. She decided wearing the parka would be easier than carrying it. She pulled it on and almost stopped breathing when the zipper zipped up with a slashing noise. She paused, wriggling her toes nervously. She wished her sneakers were not so old and broken. The little toe on her right foot stuck right out. Not the best thing for walking on the prickly floor of a pine forest. But it couldn't be helped. She didn't have any other shoes.

She held her red nightgown against her cheek and wondered what to do with it. Her grandmother had made her that too, just before she finished the quilt. It sort of matched the quilt. Grandmother had made it big as though she meant it to last forever. Jasmin almost giggled aloud in the dark attic at the thought of taking the flowing red nightgown with her to wear in the wilderness. It had frills at the neck and wrists. It was the most splendid garment she had ever had, like a queen's gown from a story book.

Grandmother had been such a romantic lady, with an old sewing machine her mother had brought from a land across the sea. Jasmin really wanted to take the nightgown. So she stuffed it inside the patchwork quilt roll. Anyhow, she would need something to put on while she washed her clothes in rivers and streams when *Her bed it was the brown heath turf, Her house was out of doors.*

She almost cried when she took a last look in the moonlight at Leroy, sleeping with his eyes not quite shut and his tongue lolling out at one side. Poor Leroy. He would miss her. He followed her everywhere. The floorboards creaked as she paused to take a last look at Marigold Lolita May, the very wild, dark two-year-old, asleep with a dirty face. Some Marigold! Jasmin's eyes smarted with tears. It was so hard to leave the cuddly children because, even though Jasmin wished her mother didn't have so many children, she loved every one of them. But it was such hard work to be the oldest child in a large family.

Leroy tossed noisily, flailing his arms and shouting strange hoarse words out of the hurt, dreaming mind that nobody could understand. Jasmin often felt frustrated because she could not figure out what Leroy was saying but she could see his thoughts struggling like prisoners behind his wild pale eyes. Creeping out of the attic, she held her breath until he settled down, then she squeezed herself and her bulky baggage down the steep ladder that was the

Stalke staircase. She felt fat and awkward in her winter parka.

She stopped at the bottom of the ladder, stood still to get used to the dim moonlight in the *for everything room*. Her father's snores crept and rumbled under the closed door of the other room. The refrigerator motor suddenly whirred. Jasmin could hear her own heart thumping. She really ought to take some food, but she didn't want to risk the sharp click of the fridge door waking her parents or disturbing the fretful Honey Angelina. Anyhow, she didn't want anything extra to carry because she was intending to walk a long way, a very long way from home that night. She tiptoed across the shadowy room, hardly breathing. Just by the door, she remembered, there was a long plastic sack with potatoes in it, round redskinned potatoes. That was what she decided to take with her. Nobody would miss a few potatoes and they would be filling and juicy.

She took one last look round her home and she saw an old straw hat on a nail by the door. Nobody ever wore that hat. It was ragged round the edges, and very old. She smiled as a bit more of the poem flashed into her mind;

> Old Meg was brave as Margaret Queen,
>   And tall as Amazon;
> An old red blanket cloak she wore;
>   A chip hat had she on.

It was as if the book in her secret pocket was speaking to her again. But whatever is a chip hat? Jasmin popped the old straw hat on her head and quietly and slowly opened the door to the sudden cool night of the outside. The moonlight was brilliant.

In the shadow of the house she slipped her arms into the rope loops and pulled the quilt up onto her shoulders like a pack. She decided it was easier to carry the long plastic bag with its few potatoes in her hand.

She would head westwards into the forest wilderness, but not go on the winding gravel road in case a truck driving home to a lonely farm discovered her in its headlights. Jasmin Marie Antoinette Stalke was a fugitive now and nobody must see her. She would go through the bush, west to the mountains.

Across the overturned cars and the spokes, wheels and handles of the rusty junk machinery, now all silver and magic in the moonlight, through a clearing in the trees, Jasmin could see the Rocky Mountains. They rose like gray giant shadows on the edge of the night. And she heard the coyotes. They were yipping and yowling and crying like ghosts round the mountains in the moonlight night.

What if she got scared?

She stuck out her chin and started walking. She was *not* going to let herself get scared.

A bat swooped down near her. It swished the air, a feathery, ghosty swishing that made Jasmin's heart pound violently in her ears and her mouth go dry. She wasn't going to let herself be afraid. She kept making herself walk on, chin up, her long shadow like a hunchbacked giant with a big spiky head, swinging a massive club, walking through the long, black shadows of the softly whispering trees.

She tried to breathe silently. Inside she was quaking. But she walked on.

For the first few miles it was Stalke land, easy traveling because for decades horses and cattle had eaten out the underbrush. Even so, whenever she came to a patch where the trees were thick and close, making shadows dark as caves, she could hardly breathe for the black fear that thudded in her chest. She kept remembering, *Old Meg was brave as Margaret Queen, And tall as Amazon.* Old Meg, *she* wouldn't be childish and afraid of the dark. So Jasmin walked on.

At the far edge of the Stalke land she came to a barbed wire fence, five tight strands, silver in the moonlight. She had to take off her pack and her parka and set them and her potatoes on the other side, which was a long open field, before she could wriggle under the bottom strand. As she pressed herself down she felt the earth cool with night dew. The coarse grasses made her hands and face wet as she squirmed flatter to the ground.

She stood up and paused to take a deep breath. From the hilltop, she looked down across wide forests and valleys between her and the mountains. The distant mountains stood dark and brooding, while the open field was white with moonlight. "It's beautiful," Jasmin murmured to herself as she looked up into the sky crowded with stars. What a lot we miss sleeping in stuffy bedrooms while the night spreads out like an adventure, she thought.

Suddenly she was filled with a magnificent feeling of courage, wild and free. She felt like twirling around and shouting out sounds of happiness to echo down the valley. She didn't do it though; she held her feelings in as she'd practiced doing ever since she could remember. She wouldn't want even the stars to suspect that the tough and sensible oldest child had lovely, silly, childish feelings inside. She just looked around and smiled.

Then, as she bent down to pick up her parka and pack, out of the corner of her eye, she saw a shadow slinking across the far end of the field. She paused and stayed bent over. Without moving, she looked sideways and saw five shadows creeping low to the ground.

Glints of moonlit eyes were watching her.

Suddenly her sneakers felt very cold and wet in the long grasses. Her fingers were stiff and icy.

Slowly, very slowly, she stood upright.

Five coyotes were silently slinking along, dragging gray shadows across the moonlight. They spread out over the field, watching her. Creeping. They never turned away from her. They were spreading round her.

She did not move.

Her feet were ice.

What could she do?

3

LEROY LORNE RAPHAEL WOKE UP AND SAW THE empty window. Only the moon stared into his eyes. He remembered there was something bad about that window. Something very bad. He could remember, now that the pill they gave him had worn off. He had done something bad. The pretty plants were gone and he had heard Jasmin crying. He had heard Jasmin crying through the drifting fog that the pills made in his mind but she was not crying now. Only the moon looked at him through the naked window. Poor pretty plants gone.

He sat up, the moonlight making gossamer of his white hair. He leaned out of his bed to find Jasmin. He couldn't see her. Frightened, he lurched out of his bed and over to hers. He touched the bed all over, unable to believe that Jasmin was not there. He looked under the pillow. He felt awkwardly round the bed and under the bed, his breathing getting more and more troubled and excited. Suddenly frantic, wearing only his underpants and barefoot, he slid down the ladder, making frightened grunting noises, trying to call Jasmin. Her name couldn't get any further than his throat. His short-legged body lurched heavily across the *for everything room* and out the door. It banged behind him and he stumbled into the tin bath that hung like a

19

long coffin on the outside wall by the door. The crashing tin bath sounded like a hollow drum booming in the night. Then it banged and clattered down off its hook and fell across some empty oil drums till the noise was like a wild battle. One oil drum went rolling and bumping, rumbling and racketing, bouncing on roots and rocks and finally bashing up against an old hunk of machinery. Leroy ran without noticing, panting out his strange hoarse cry, calling for Jasmin, his sister who listened to him.

"What the! What the devil's going on?" Bud Stalke was suddenly out of bed and shouting at the open door. His gun clicked sharply as he loaded it. He was stark naked in the moonlight.

Olive, Jasmin's mother, came up sleepily behind him yawning and sighing. She was hugging a tight shiny pink nightie to her body because of the night chill. "Whatever was it, Bud?" she whispered as she peered out the door. "Is it a bear?"

Bud stepped out bravely into the bright moonlight, his gun at the ready. He narrowed his eyes, scanning the dark shadows among the trees and old cars and machinery. Olive reached into the house and got a coat from one of the nails behind the door. She shivered and put the short coat on over her nightie. "Look here, Bud," she said. "Give me the gun. I'll look around. You go get some clothes on. You could catch your death like that. And what would anybody think if they came up and saw you like that. You sure do look funny." Olive laughed and pointed her finger. Her deep laughter rang out in the night.

Bud let her take the gun from his hands. "I sure don't smell no bear," he said sniffing as he went indoors.

"And it sure ain't like a deer to be coming this close in," Olive said to herself as she rubbed her plump cheek against the smooth wood of the gun stock.

"You know, I thought I heard the door open and bang," Bud said as he came out again pushing his shirt down inside his snug jeans, then shoving his bare feet down into his pointed cowboy boots.

"Knocked the bath down, whatever it was. Must have been something big and strong," Olive said as she peered round the side of the house. "But reckon I don't see nothing."

"Shut up woman. Stop your gabbing a minute and listen, will you," Bud said irritably with his head to one side. In the silence they heard the coyotes calling against the faraway sky. Not so far away there were strange gasping grunting cries. They seemed to come from the road beyond the upside down cars and junk.

"Listen, Bud. Whatever's that?" Olive set the gun down.

"Muv. Muv. Dad." A sleepy voice from behind startled them and two little hands clutched behind their legs. It was five-year-old Carmen Miranda Elisa, a tiny one with hair as pale and silky as a dandelion's clock.

"Oh, sweetie, sweetie pie, did the nasty noise wake you then." Olive comforted the little one, picking her up and rocking her in her big arms.

"Leroy gone," the little girl said sleepily and pointed to the road. "Leroy gone undressed."

"Oh, forever more! It's him again, is it?" Bud grumbled. "Him having one of his funny fits again. Might have known. Why isn't Jasmin keeping an eye on him, I'd like to know."

"Oh dear. That is what that funny noise is. It *is* Leroy, bless him. It's after him having that bad fright jumping out the window. We should have known. He really hit hard when he fell off that rope." Olive was almost crying and she began to run toward the road hugging little Carmen Miranda Elisa to her warm soft body as she ran.

Impatiently Bud unloaded the gun and set it inside the door muttering to himself, "I'll give 'em Tarzan." He ran and caught up with Olive who was calling into the night, "Leroy love, where are you? Leroy, Leroy. Leroy love."

"I'll give him love, when I get my hands on him," Bud threatened as he paused to wipe his forehead.

"There he is. There he is, bless him," Olive panted and tried to go faster. They could see the stumbling figure of Leroy, moonlight on his white hair, running with his arms flailing toward the western mountains.

They caught up with him and turned him round so he was facing back home. Bud kept pushing him unsympathetically while Olive tried to be kind and to encourage him along. Little Carmen Miranda Elisa had gone to sleep, very heavy in her mother's arms.

"Now be a good boy. Take your pill and you'll feel better." Olive humored poor Leroy when he was back in the *for everything room.*

Leroy kept trying to tell them that Jasmin had gone because he had hurt her plants. He waved his arms excitedly, harsh noises bursting out instead of words. He struggled when they tried to push the pills into his mouth, those pills that took his thoughts away. He fought until Bud pinned him down on the floor, pushed two pills into his mouth and held his nose until he had to swallow. Two pills together were very strong. They soon made Leroy calm down and, through the fog of his drugged mind, he did as he was told quietly. He settled down to sleep on the bumpy big chesterfield while his parents took Carmen Miranda Elisa into their bed so no more of the children would be awakened.

Soon the house was quiet again, everyone sleeping peacefully, while the silent moon sailed overhead and the coyotes called like lonely ghosts haunting the western night.

Leroy was the only one who knew that Jasmin was out there alone in the vast night.

4

THE GRAY COYOTE SHADOWS WITH THE GLINTING EYES crept across the field, watching Jasmin. Suddenly the outdoors felt enormous and she felt very, very small, alone against the barbed wire fence on the east side of the field with her pack and her bag with its few potatoes. She shuddered, cold to the bone, easing and wriggling her toes in her soggy, dew-soaked sneakers. She thought wildly, *this isn't like it is on TV. On TV girls get superhuman courage when they're in danger. Or somebody appears to save them.* All that was happening to her was that she was plain scared and beginning to tremble. But she had to do something. She couldn't just do nothing.

Slowly, furtively, she picked up the long plastic sack with the potatoes at the bottom. In her mind she saw a picture of herself swinging it round and round, keeping the snarling, raging coyotes off with it, like the Three Musketeers on TV. But there was only one of her.

Although she could hardly breathe, her mind was rushing and leaping every which way. It was telling her that now she would be saved from failing her grade. She'd be dead instead. Everybody would be sorry. Even the worst teacher wouldn't fail a dead student. Now, she'd have a good excuse for not getting a science project done. At school they would put her name on a gold sign outside the principal's office next to the honor roll—*To the Memory of Jasmin Marie Antoinette Stalke, R.I.P.* Everybody would be sorry. She would be remembered. All the men would go out with guns to hunt the raging coyotes down.

But while her make-believe mind was seeing herself torn to pieces and everybody crying and sorry, Jasmin's practical mind was telling her that coyotes don't attack people. Her mother would say the same as she always said when a bear was near, "Sing, Jasmin, sing. That's enough to frighten anything off when you sing. Anyhow, wild animals are more afraid of you than you are of them."

Jasmin took a big, trembling breath to try to make herself calm inside. The coyotes went on staring. Jasmin found enough courage from somewhere to try to be normal.

"Hi." She pushed out a small word as an experiment. The sound was little and sharp across the moonlit field and it trembled down the vast black valley.

The coyotes stopped quite still. They tilted their heads and listened. Alert.

"It's only me." Jasmin tried a few more words. The coyotes held quite still. "I'm just walking this way, that's all." When she'd said that she giggled nervously. She felt silly and self-conscious, crazy, a girl in the big night talking to coyotes. The coyotes remained still, their bushy tails hanging, their shadows stretching in front of them long as monsters.

Jasmin was getting braver every second. She was still alive wasn't she? She went on talking, and gradually, careful not to make a sudden movement, she slid into her parka and eased her pack onto her shoulders. "I'm not going to hurt anything. Honest. I don't have a gun. Not even a knife. I'm coming to live here too." As she talked she tried moving, slow step by slow step, toward the watching eyes.

25

Her giant, hunchbacked shadow walked with her. She kept on talking, trying to sound calm while her heart thudded in her ears and almost burst her chest.

The coyotes paused a few seconds longer. Then they slowly turned and with silent dignity, following their leader, they trotted away to the far fence and disappeared into the deep shadow of the forest.

What a relief! Jasmin laughed, but her legs were trembling and her insides quivering. She shouted across the field to the dark place where the coyotes had disappeared, "I'm only a girl. I'm just as afraid as you are."

"Too-whoo, too-whoo." A big owl swooped low in a quick tremble of air, making Jasmin's stomach dive and plunge again in another spasm of fear. "Too-whoo, too-whooo." The owl wheeled and glided away down the field repeating its sounds as though it were laughing sadly. Jasmin got mad at herself for being frightened by a night owl. She called after it, "Too-whoo to you tooo. Did you have to scare me too? You silly ghost thing. Creeping up on a person like that!"

Then she stood quite still and listened to the quiet that fell when her own words stopped. She was breathless with relief, but also feeling triumphant, pleased with herself. Now she felt marvelously strong and tough. She had just won a battle against her own fear. She looked at her shadow, a terrible spooky thing, and she stretched out her arms and made witchy scratching fingers to claw at the moonlit earth. Crazy. Crazy. She made her monster shadow creep crazily and she shrieked like a witch, like a wild creature in the night, "Yeeee—yahoooo, yeeeeooooooooooo."

There was nobody to tell her to shut up and act her age. Out in the wilderness she could do weird and wild and childish things if she wanted to. Out in the wilderness she didn't have to be the sensible oldest child. "Yeeeeeoooooooo."

So who was afraid?

She marched confidently and exultantly across the moonbright field toward the silver fence on the west side. She marched to a little tune in her head that was singing, "Westwards, to live, westwards, *she lived as she did please, she lived as she did please,* Oh, Jasmin Marie Antoinette Stalke, *she lived as she did please, O,*"

5

JASMIN WAS TO LEARN HOW QUICKLY THE WILDERNESS could change her mood; when she reached the west fence on the other side of the moonlit field she lost her courage again. Pitch black forest crowded up to the tight strands of the barbed wire fence. She walked slowly along the fenceline, trying to find a place to crawl under, somewhere with a break in the thick underbrush of willows and prickly rosebushes on the other side, a place where deer had made a pathway. She had reached a place where the forest was truly wild, where it had never been tamed by man or thinned out by cows, sheep, and horses grazing.

At last she found a spot to wriggle under, with her parka on, and she stood up on the wild side. She slipped her arms back into her pack ropes and pulled her hat well down on her head. Then she stood, just stood there. It was scary. She stared into the tree-breathing darkness, too scared to move. It smelled earthy and secret in there, different from the lovely summer fragrance of the open grassy field under the big starlit sky. It was terribly quiet in there. There was the warm musk smell of deer. It was terrifyingly black.

She wondered how she could ever make herself plunge into that close and frightening darkness. She didn't want to do it.

"It isn't fair. It isn't fair," she murmured desperately to herself. Why did she have to do this terrifying thing just because of her silly brothers and sisters and her silly homework and her silly science project and her silly teachers? It wasn't fair. Her throat went thick with wanting to cry. It wasn't fair.

But she had no choice; she made herself take the first few steps gingerly along the deer trail. Then she paused. Her eyes, getting accustomed to the blackness, began to see in the trail ahead the white gleam of a poplar's bark where the moonlight had found a way in through the tall treetops. And she began to see a sprinkling of light, like lacy patterns on the forest floor, where bits of the bright night sky had fallen through.

The track was very narrow and, as she moved along it, twigs pulled at her jeans and snagged on her quilt pack. A springy branch almost grabbed off her hat. She had to keep her head down so thin branches didn't lash across her eyes. And what a noise she was making! She was like her own private earthquake, disturbing the black silence: crash, crash. Her feet surged through the forest floor of deep and ancient pine needles. Old branches cracked and snapped. Thin young branches swooshed. When she stopped, the intense silence crushed in again, seeming loud in her ears as she struggled to get free of a broken branch that had got caught up her jean leg. She was sweating inside her winter parka.

A person could get lost in a forest like this, Jasmin thought fearfully, as she struggled to get her leg free and still hold on to her potatoes. But how could she get lost when she was not going home again? Surely you can only get lost if there's a special place you have to find. How could she get lost when all she wanted to do was to get away, just far away westwards? But she would have to be careful that she didn't simply go round in circles. She must be sure to keep going downhill, because between her and the mountains there was a river in a wide valley.

She got her jean leg free and crashed on again, pushing her way downwards through the low branches stretching across the narrow trail. Pine needles kept working their way in through the hole in her sneaker where her little toe stuck out. Eventually, it got so uncomfortable that she had to take off her sneaker and shake it out. She sat with her back to the white bark of a thick tree trunk that was glimmering with moonlight. She hadn't bothered to untie her shoelace and was struggling to get her foot back in when a piercing scream made her stop breathing.

The scream was like a sharp knife cutting through her heart. Before Jasmin could take a breath there was another scream, then another. Horror and pain shredded the darkness. Some animal was dying horribly in the forest, hunted down—by what killer? She shuddered and pressed her back against the tree, her eyes searching the darkness as the cries went on and on. There were three quick, desperate, small, shrill cries in quick succession. Then trembling silence. The memory of the screams echoed on in Jasmin's ears. Some animal was dead.

Jasmin crouched and looked around the dark branches for eyes, crouched low to the earth and could not move. She felt the hunted animal's desperation trembling inside her. She stayed bent over, down near the earth, for what seemed an eternity, waiting for her breathing to come to order.

Then, slowly, watching the terrible menacing darkness, she stood up and started off to walk again through the grabbing fingers of the branches.

"Old Meg was brave as Margaret Queen," she whispered to herself and told herself to keep going, to push on downwards, downwards into the valley.

Twice again as she crashed and stumbled through the night she was soul-sickened and terrified by the cries of animals dying violently, surprised by killers. Were silent killers waiting to pounce on her? Would she scream like that?

She got so hot she had to stop to unzip her parka, and the sound of the zipper was like a saw blade rasping. She shuddered as she plodded and crashed on, holding in her fear.

The night and the forest began to seem endless. She was exhausted, her legs aching, her eyes wanting to sleep. It seemed such a long time ago since she had packed the little kids' lunch pails, failed her social studies test, gone home to find her science project ruined, made supper, put the little kids to bed, stayed awake in the moonlight by her window, waiting for the Stalke house to go to sleep. If only she could go to sleep now. She was finding it harder and harder to stay on the trail and not stagger off it like a drunken man. She began to think that the dark ahead of her was growing paler. Was it really growing paler or was she dreaming? Surely it was beginning to look lighter. She had to pause to catch her breath, to cool down. She stumbled toward a big poplar tree and leaned her face against its cool, silver bark. She reached her hands upwards and spread them on the rough safeness of the solid, friendly tree. But this time silence did not fall around her.

There was a snapping of twigs, a rustling in the pine-needled floor that she was not making. She pulled herself tight against the tree trunk. She could guess what that snapping and crashing was, because she knew the smell that was rising in the forest. It was a smell like a thousand old sweaty socks. An old male bear. That's what it was. Her mind cried, *Danger. Terrible danger.*

Quickly, in her panic, she slung the potato bag as far as she could down the trail. Anybody knew that a bear would go after any sort of food, so she had to get those potatoes well away from herself. But what else could she do to save herself? Her mind was racing. It was no good trying to climb the tree. She knew that a bear with its long, strong claws could climb any tree quicker and better than she could. She gasped and hung onto the rough, cool tree, hugging it with her upstretched arms. If she were to run, it would be just like a cat with a mouse. The bear could pounce on her and play with her if he wanted to. Where could she run to anyhow? Would she scream like those other animals? The smell got sickeningly closer. She pushed her mouth hard against the silver bark. The crashing and rustling stopped. Jasmin did not breathe. Then there were little coughing grunts, very near her, behind her. Her chest felt as though it would burst against the tree. Her stomach was turning and her bladder crawling. The little grunting coughs kept on.

She had to control her breathing. She had to know what was happening. She clasped the tree tightly as if it were going to save her, hold her up. Slowly, horribly slowly, she turned her head a bit, then a bit more until, out of the corner of her eye, she could see the dark form of the bear, a big shadowy bulk against the white bark of a tree trunk. He was reaching up his tree as Jasmin was reaching up hers, arms raised, hugging it. He was reaching up and making the grunting sounds.

She held on tight. Now what was she supposed to do? Her mother would say, "Sing, Jasmin, sing. That's enough to frighten anything off." But she didn't feel like singing. Instead, she hugged the tree harder and with her face half pressed against it, half watching the big shadow of the black bear, she said the first thing that came into her head very fast and trembly and all joined together. *"Old Meg was brave as Margaret Queen and tall as Amazon an old red blanket cloak she wore a chip hat had she on."*

The bear went quite still. The grunting stopped.

A chip hat had she on, Jasmin repeated a bit more firmly.

The bear grunted and reached higher up the tree.

"Okay. You win. You can reach higher than I can," Jasmin said bravely. Then, to give herself more courage, added, *"A chip hat had she on."* The bear kept very still, so she said it again, louder, almost shouting. *"A CHIP HAT HAD SHE ON."* What a ridiculous thing to say to a bear in a forest, her mind said to her. But it seemed to be working. The bear seemed to listen and take it seriously. Her mother would say, "Wild animals are more feared of you than you are of them." Her mother seemed to know a lot of things about nature. Perhaps a girl should listen to her mother, Jasmin thought. She usually felt very critical of her big fat mother but

33

perhaps her mother did have some good points. She'd be sorry if her daughter got killed by a bear. What a funny thing to be thinking about when she was in danger, so near a big old bear. Anyhow, she hoped her mother would be sorry now her oldest child had run away. But that didn't matter, did it? Her mother had lots more children to care about. *"A chip hat had she on, a chip hat had she on,"* Jasmin said to the bear as though she were saying it crossly to her mother. She let go the tree and turned to face his big smelly back. She clapped her hands sharply and said as though she were ending an argument, "I'm not staying here. I know this is your place." She clapped her hands again and the sound cracked loud through the forest.

The bear grunted like an old man. He turned around and gave her one tired look, just as her mother would at the end of an argument. Then he ambled off into the bush, luckily in the opposite direction to the way she was going.

So, her mother was right. The bear had been afraid of her too. But she was still trembling. She turned round to face the friendly tree again, to hold on to its big strong coolness. She had not wet herself, but she wanted to cry, or go to sleep. She was so tired, so very tired.

When the smell had lessened and sounds of the bear snapping twigs had faded in the distance, she moved on, finding her potato bag along the trail. The forest was no longer silent. There were the dawn sounds of birds awakening. All around her were little chirps and chirrups of life. There was a paler edge to the trees now. She felt sure she must be nearing the river. She stumbled on, almost asleep on her feet. She was too tired to be afraid of anything anymore. She was too tired for *anything*. She *had* to sleep, so she pushed her way off the deer trail and crawled until she found a place to lie down in the underbrush. She rolled herself up in her patchwork quilt, put her cheek on her folded red nightgown, and immediately she was asleep.

Jasmin Marie Antoinette Stalke, the girl who was failing, was a very small rolled-up patchwork bundle among the thick willows in a great big forest. While she slept, too tired for dreaming, the coyotes were calling, making spooky, high-pitched sounds in the empty skies.

6

THE ALARM CLOCK SHRILLED ON THE FLOOR BY BUD Stalke's side of the bed. Sleepily he pushed his pillow down over it to muffle the ringing and he went right back to his dream where he was the famous rodeo cowboy riding out of a chute on a wild bucking bronco. In his dream he was waving his black cowboy hat and the crowd was roaring. In his dream, he was the hero, the winner.

Carmen Miranda Elisa snuggled warmly up to her mother who slept smiling and untroubled with one arm stretched across to Honey Angelina's crib.

On the chesterfield in the other room, Leroy half-heard the alarm, jerked his arms upwards as he tried to sit up, crying out mixed-up words. Then he fell back again, his hair very white and his skin a pale pink against the greasy plum color of the old chesterfield. He fell back into an uneasy sleep where he was running through spiders' webs, pushing them out of his eyes, out of his mouth, pulling them off his eyelashes. His head flopped from side to side.

In the attic nobody was stirring. Marigold Lolita May, her face still dirty, was in Merron Damion Hugh's bed where she'd crawled in the middle of the night because a mouse had run across her bed and scared her. Although Merron was only six, thin and small for his age, he seemed like a big strong brother to her.

Eglantine Sophia, the nine-year-old who looked like Jasmin, had gone to sleep with her glasses on the end of her nose. They wobbled as she snored.

Nathanial Augustus John smiled in his sleep like a Valentine card angel.

While all the Stalke family went on sleeping and dreaming, brown squirrels chased up and down their sloping roof, chittering in the cool bright morning.

Sunshine glimmered on Jasmin's empty bed.

It was a quarter past seven when the alarm first rang, the time to be up if the school-age children were to catch the van on the road at twenty past eight.

It was past eight o'clock when suddenly a great

36

commotion shattered the peaceful morning. A bull bellowed like a squalling trumpet, then a chorus of cows mooed in a loud concert of consternation.

"Yippee!" Bud Stalke woke up waving his arms and spurring his wild bronco. He thought he was still in his dream with the crowd roaring until he opened his eyes.

"Aw shucks," he moaned when he realized that the roaring crowd was only cows. But he was out of bed in an instant, pushing himself into his clothes shouting, "Aw shucks, Olive, willya listen to that racket?"

Olive smiled without opening her eyes.

"Olive, will yer listen? Them rotten cattle is out on the road agin. That's all we need—to get one of 'em hit by a truck. Olive, are yer listening?"

Olive cuddled Carmen Miranda Elisa closer to her and said, "Uum-uum," without opening her eyes.

Bud picked up the pillow crossly and swore through his teeth when he saw the face of the alarm clock. Then he cried out, "Shucks, shucks, shucks, Olive. It's gone eight o'clock. Better get moving."

He went and yelled up the ladder, "Get moving, you kids. It's late," then rushed off, stuffing his black hat on his rumpled head, mumbling and grumbling that he was sick to death of rotten cattle that were always breaking through fences.

Up in the attic pandemonium broke loose.

Merron Damion Hugh pushed Marigold Lolita May onto the floor so he could search in the bed for his T-shirt and socks. She screamed so loud that

Eglantine jumped out of bed in shock. Her glasses bounced off her nose and she stepped on them.

"Jasmin," she called out furiously, "Now look what you've made me do. Why don't you stop these kids making such a noise." Eglantine groped on the floor among jeans and sneakers and her homework books to find the arm of her glasses that had broken off.

Nathaniel Augustus John was throwing everybody else's clothes about trying to find his jeans. "Jasmin," he called out plaintively, "I can't find anything to wear. I can't go to school like this."

"Come on, you kids," Olive called sleepily up the ladder, "The bus'll be here any minute."

Marigold Lolita May was the first to slide down the ladder in her skimpy nightshirt. She rushed past her mother, across the room, out into the morning, leaving the back door wide open.

"Put something on them feet," Olive shouted as Marigold ran along the dew-wet pathway to the outhouse.

A crowd of gaudy bantam hens rushed to the open door, clucking and cackling their demand for breakfast.

Carmen Miranda Elisa staggered out from her mother's warm bed and put the TV on very loud and sat down two feet in front of it. Now anybody who wanted to be heard would have to shout over TV.

Honey Angelina started bawling.

Nathaniel Augustus John came down the ladder in a pair of Eglantine's jeans that were too big for him. "If you tell Mom, I'll tell her you broke your glasses and she'll kill you," he warned his sister.

She put her broken glasses inside her homework binder and came down the ladder with it carefully. Then she got into a fight with Nathaniel because he wanted to wash first in the tin bowl by the front door.

"It doesn't matter. Don't mind me," she shouted at him. "I can go to school without washing." She snatched up the comb and ran away with it so he wouldn't be able to comb his hair.

Merron Damion Hugh started crying because he'd got a knot in his shoelace and couldn't get his sneaker on.

In all the noise and chaos, Leroy tried to stand up but fell back babbling.

Olive, cheerful and unperturbed, smiled across all the goings-on and shouted up the ladder, "Jasmin. Jasmin love. Where are you, Jasmin? Jasmin love, you'll have to be quick and fix the lunch pails. Come on, be quick, before the bus gets here."

Jasmin didn't answer.

Leroy tried to get up again, waving his arms excitedly and making sounds toward his mother. He was trying to tell her—but those pills still muddled his thoughts and he lost them. He sat down on the edge of the chesterfield, leaned back and nodded off to sleep with his eyes not quite closed and his tongue slipping out at one side.

Olive grew impatient as she called again. "Are you trying to make me mad, Jasmin? It's not like you to make trouble for your mother. Answer me. Answer me. Do you hear? Answer me or—or—" Olive, with her sloppy pink slippers flipping, huffed and puffed up the ladder until her head was looking into the attic. She couldn't go any further. She was too fat.

"Well!" she burst out. "Holy shucks, what a mess! I never seen such a mess in my born days. It's a pigsty up here. Jasmin. What d'you think you've been doing, letting the kids make a mess like this?" She raised her voice shrilly above all the noises, held on the ladder with one hand and wagged a finger at all the children downstairs. "Youse guys, when youse all get home from school you can all get up here and clean the pigsty up." She pushed her head into the attic again, poking it further in to peer around and carry on. "And you, Jasmin, are you listening? I'm surprised at you, the oldest, letting it get into a mess like this. Jasmin, are you listening to me?"

Nathaniel Augustus John swung round the bottom of the ladder, cheekily shaking his black curls and twinkling his innocent blue eyes in his chubby face. "T'aint no good yelling," he called up to his mother. "Jasmin ain't up there. She weren't up there when we come down."

"Aw holy shucks, then why didn't somebody tell me instead of youse all letting me be a fool talking to myself." Olive laughed, good-natured again. "I can just guess what that girl's done," she chuckled. "Wouldn't you just know it! She'll have slipped out with her Dad to get the cattle back in. Anything to miss school. What a girl! Come on, Eglantine. Guess you'll have to get over here and fix the lunch pails while I see to the baby."

"That's not fair, Jasmin's supposed to fix the lunch pails," Eglantine grumbled. "I'm going to be late already."

"Now quit your grumbling, willya." Olive gave Eglantine a push toward the refrigerator. "Put your glasses on and see what you can find, there's a good girl. Your dad most likely needed a hand rounding up them cattle. Jasmin can't be in two places at once, can she now?"

"Jasmin's crazy," Eglantine said to Nathaniel when at last they rushed out and onto the schoolbus. "She's already been warned two times that she's going to fail if she misses any more days."

"Guess she'll be in real bad trouble this time," Nathaniel said.

"Serves her right. It'll stop her from being so stuck up," Eglantine said. "And don't you dare tell Mom when you get home that you just got dry bread sandwiches. I'll kill you if you do."

"Aw, Eg—you! And I never told you'd broke your glasses. Aw, Eg," Nathaniel moaned as he flopped in his seat after looking in his lunch pail. "I sure hope Jasmin fixes lunch pails tomorrow."

41

7

A MIST OF SILVER DEW HAD SETTLED ON THE BRIL-
liant reds, blues, and yellows of the curled up patchwork cocoon among the willows below a spruce tree.
Springy branches bounced and swayed as agile
brown squirrels chased along them chattering
noisily.

The cocoon stirred, stretched itself out, surpris-
ing the squirrels who scurried to the topmost
branches to carry on their noisy grumbling.

With one finger, Jasmin pushed the snug goose
feather warmth from one eye and looked warily up
through the patterns of leaves and twigs and spreading branches. Far away at the top of the pattern she
saw bits of a very blue sky. She breathed contentedly.
Her first morning, and she was snug, comfortable
and safe. Luxuriously she stretched her legs, wriggled her toes that were stiff but warm inside her
sneakers. Then she lifted her entire face out into
the morning.

"Ooh," she gasped, for the air was chill. She
sniffed in the scent of the forest air that was like
honey and Christmas trees. She took in a full breath
of the freshness and then breathed out a long sigh
of contentment. Besides the argumentative squirrels,
birds were calling and twittering everywhere. A

vivid blue jay landed on a branch almost by her nose, then flashed away.

Jasmin snuggled in the warmth of her quilt and thought happily, *Her bed it was the brown heath turf. Her house was out of doors.* This outdoor waking-up was even better than waking up had been when the sun shone through the leaves of her plants on the window ledge, making trembly shadows on her bed and sometimes on Leroy's face and pillow, while she lay thinking before all the little kids woke up.

She decided that waking up in the forest morning was the best thing she'd ever done in her life. She didn't have to get up because nobody needed her. She relaxed into the lovely warmth, lay back to look upwards through the patterns of the branches. She watched the soft, pale undersides of squirrels and twittering, flitting groups of tiny chickadees.

What an interesting way to see things, she thought, looking up.

Perhaps she would stay all day just watching the underside view of things with the sky shining blue as jewels through the quivering branches. This morning she could *live as she did please.* It was the first morning in the first day of her new life. This morning she didn't have to wash little faces, tie up shoe laces, or fix lunch pails. Nobody was yelling, "Jasmin do this, Jasmin do that."

Today there would be no tests to fail.

Already, she was glad she had run away. It was a very special feeling to be alone and free in the forest morning.

Her thoughts were interrupted. Somewhere, just off to the right of where she lay, there was a crunching and a rustling in the pine-needled underbrush.

She lay quite still, only moving her face slightly to see what it was, but her heart did not beat with fear as it had in the darkness. In the morning light the menace of the forest seemed to have gone away.

Very slowly, the rustling drew near her, then nearer until she saw a lurching, fat ball of a porcupine, crossing the bright dapples of sunshine. Its bristles, touched by the sun, were amber. From down where she was, Jasmin looked up into its sad little gray face with its dim, mild eyes.

For some unknown reason, that face reminded her of Leroy, merrily lurching and shining in the sunshine. Jasmin shivered. It was terrible to get Leroy mixed up with the porcupine in her thoughts. She hated it when her father had to shoot porcupines because they slung their spines into the cattle. The porcupine faces were so sad and hopeless when they looked down from trees they had climbed. Her father would raise his gun. Bang. The porcupine would drop down dead. No shine left, just a dead hunk of prickles. Her father would skin off the spines and her mother would cook the meat. It tasted like chicken.

She studied the porcupine as its little feet brought its armed body closer and closer. Maybe, she speculated, she would have to kill and eat porcupine now she was a fugitive.

No sooner did she think of food than she began to feel hungry. She sat up to scrutinize the forest floor, startling the porcupine who moved just a little quicker, turning away from her. It's movement, even as it hurried, was still so slow that Jasmin thought, Well, I could easily catch a porcupine. But how would I kill it? The thought repelled her.

Clearly, she might have to kill things to eat. The forest floor didn't look any too promising; mostly old dry pine needles, a bit dampened on the top layer by the morning dew. Not a thing in sight to nibble on—except the porcupine.

"Um," Jasmin said to herself, "you had better start facing up to the day's problems. You can't just lie here enjoying yourself. You, my girl, are going to get hungry."

And with the wide-awake thought of hunger there came the thought that somebody could already be looking for her because, by now, they would have found out that her bed was empty and the quilt missing.

"See," she said sorrowfully to herself, "you can't lie late in bed until you've found a place to hide. And it's got to be a place where nobody will find you. Nobody, see. So, get moving," she ended up sternly, adding her voice to the other chattering and twittering creatures in the tree. Talking to herself was beginning to seem quite normal.

Shiveringly, she made herself get out of her snug cocoon and shake out her quilt, which was wet with dew. Her splendid red gown was a crumpled mess because she had used it as a pillow. She rolled the damp quilt and the creased gown together as quickly as she could. Then, with her pack on her back, chewing on a juicy red potato, she started off again on her journey down the narrow deer trail.

Soon she was humming and thinking that this was how explorers must have walked through the land looking for places to settle. She laughed and began to say over to herself things she had learned in social studies about settlements.

"It must be near water for drinking and washing."

"It must be near a source of food."

"It must provide a dry place for sleeping, safe from enemies and wild animals."

She couldn't remember if the last two were really in the social studies lessons or whether she was making those up to suit her own needs. She began to hurry as the thought of finding her own hiding-home excited her.

"I can't remember going anywhere by myself—except to the outhouse," she said and giggled happily. Even as she enjoyed her happiness, she thought of Leroy lurching along by her side. He'd stop to watch a beetle or a caterpillar, kneel behind it, following it with his thick finger, making strange noises of conversation.

Suddenly Jasmin felt awful for not bringing Leroy with her. She could hear her mother's voice crying out, "Don't be so selfish, Jasmin. Take Marigold. Take Carmen Miranda. Take Nathaniel. Take

Merron." Her mother never had to yell, "Take Leroy." Leroy always followed her—sometimes to the outhouse.

"I should have brought him with me," she said aloud, but her mind was thinking it wasn't fair. I could never have a friend, or stay overnight. Eglantine had a friend because she wasn't always dragging little kids around with her.

"I ought to have made a pack to carry the babies," she said as she thought how much easier the pack on her back was than her usual load of a heavy baby in her arms.

"If ever I have children, I'll have just one so there won't be an oldest." She marched to the sound of her own voice.

"Or maybe I'll have twins, then there won't be an oldest." As her voice spoke those words she wondered if Leroy would have been like a friend if he hadn't been retarded. Leroy was always coming into her mind. Even in the forest, she couldn't stop worrying about him. In fact, even though she was anxious to find her own hiding-home, she couldn't stop worrying about her family.

"I hope Eglantine is looking after them. She will have to be the oldest now."

Lost in her thoughts, she went on struggling downwards toward the valley on the deer trail that turned and twisted. Twigs and thorns tugged at her jeans and hat and snagged her parka. She moved with urgency because somebody could be searching for her, following her trail.

47

8

"OH, EGLANTINE STALKE, JUST RUN AND FIND JAS-
min. I need to talk to her—seriously," Jasmin's
teacher called out as he passed her on his way
through the school doors. Eglantine was trying to
get in before school started to get some tape to fix
the arm on her glasses because she couldn't see the
blackboard without them.

"No, you can't come in," the teacher on duty
behind the door told her without giving her a chance
to explain what she needed to do. "Nobody's allowed
in. Not until the bell goes. Go away and play until
the bell goes."

It was bad enough having her glasses broken
without being bothered about Jasmin. She knew
that the teachers would ask, "Where's Jasmin?"
again. Then Mr. Podluck, the principal, would send
for her and she'd get a lecture because Jasmin was
playing hookey. As though it was her fault Jasmin
was always missing school! If Merron Damion Hugh
had wakened Jasmin instead of her she would never
have trodden on her glasses.

"Why aren't you wearing your glasses, Eglantine?" That was her teacher asking.

"I need to come in and get some tape to fix
them."

"Oh, come on then. You Stalke kids! If it isn't

48

one thing then it's another." The teacher laughed. She didn't mean to be unkind but her words made Eglantine more sulky than ever.

When she was halfway along the corridor Jasmin's teacher saw her again.

"Did you tell Jasmin to come and see me?" he asked.

But before Eglantine had a chance to answer, her teacher was saying she needed some suitable tape to make a good job of mending *this child*'s glasses, and Eglantine sensed the two teachers exchanging a long glance across her head. She remembered self-consciously that she hadn't washed her face or been to the mirror to do her hair that morning.

Jasmin's teacher found some black tape and twisted it skillfully around the broken arm of the glasses while Eglantine and her teacher watched.

"That should hold for today, but they'll need repairing properly," the teacher said as he put the glasses on Eglantine's short straight nose. "You tell your sister to come to me immediately," he said. "I need to talk to that young lady."

"Okay." Eglantine looked at the floor. "Thanks for mending my glasses," was all she muttered. Let them find out for themselves that Jasmin had stayed home. She didn't intend to get bawled out for that.

"I bet that's another one who didn't do her homework last night," her teacher said and the other agreed with a shrug.

"And she'll be able to prove that her glasses were broken. I wonder what excuse Miss Jasmin

49

Marie Antoinette will have. Excuses! Excuses! What a family."

9

JASMIN LIFTED HER ARMS AND DID A GRACEFUL DANCE, twirling around with her potatoes. At last she was out in the bright sunshine, out of the thick bush, hot inside her parka, and her jeans soaked up to the knees in dew. She had reached the margin of the forest where sunlight danced too in the leaves of the quivering aspens. As she whirled and twirled on her way, wild pink roses pulled at her with their thorns reminding Jasmin of precious *Old Meg* inside her lining.

"Her wine was dew of the wild white rose," Jasmin sang out, "and mine shall be—dew of the wild pink rose. There's enough dew to get drunk on.

Everywhere dew glistened like jewels on the delicate petals, enchanting Jasmin until she forgot she was in a hurry. She paused to smell a rose, then to taste a dew drop, then to watch a ladybug, then to pick an inchworm off her sleeve and settle it on a rose petal.

"Inchworm, where are you going?" she asked. "Why don't you stay on the petal and keep off the thorns, silly, silly? Oh, I know! Your enemies can't see you, green on green."

Enemies! That reminded her to stop dawdling.

"Goodbye. I've got enemies too. I could be in danger right now." She reminded herself that her father could come riding to find her, urging his horse quickly down the trails where she had struggled so slowly.

"Not exactly enemies. They'll be missing me at home and worrying. Can people who worry about you be your enemies?" she asked herself.

"They are never, never going to find me," she muttered determinedly and put her chin out as she imagined herself caught and taken back like a silly child, everybody knowing she was failing, all the kids at school mocking. She thought wildly that perhaps her father had already got the police out. She remembered that once, when a small plane crashed near the mountains, helicopters had roared and hovered all over the place where she was now, expertly searching.

"Hurry. Must hurry," she urged herself on.

But even her fear and urgency could not take away her sense of happy aloneness. She trailed her fingers through the feathery tops of grasses and touched soft rose petals as she passed, and she hummed to herself. Through the broken brim of her hat, the sun sprinkled gold sparkles that danced on her eyelashes, teased her on her nose, and played on her hand when she tried to catch them. Sometimes she did a little twirl around because she was full of such dancing, singing feelings.

"Hurry. Hurry. Find a hiding-home," she sang to herself, *"Alone with her great family, she lived as she did please. Alone, Alone—"*

When a hawk began to swoop down her pathway, following her, she felt uncomfortable. It swooped over her, then glided off in a wide circle, then swooped back and hovered directly above her. Birds and squirrels, in the thin aspens, called noisy warnings to each other, placing Jasmin right in the middle of a disturbance that would clue in any searcher to the presence of some passing stranger. She realized it wasn't going to be easy to move secretly in the wilderness.

"Go away," she yelled to the crazy hawk. "Go away. You're advertising that I'm here. Please pretend you haven't seen me. You're not being my friend!"

She had yelled up into the sky, her loud voice sounding strange, out of tune with the concert of wild noises. Funny, she thought, all the other noises simply fitted together to make nature's great wide silence.

Funny, too, how bits of school flashed into her thinking. "That's a paradox," she murmured, discovering its real meaning for the first time. "A paradox. All the noises make a silence."

"Go away. Please go away," she called again, but the hawk only teased her, and spread its wings, wide and luxuriously, to glide around her. She swung her potato sack up at it which only made it glide nearer. She heard the echo of her voice. She mustn't run the risk of making such loud sounds. A new thought suddenly struck her.

"Will I forget how to talk when I've lived by myself for a very long time?" she whispered, almost frightened by the idea.

"Can a person think without talking?" She asked the question out loud, and answered firmly, "Leroy does, doesn't he?"

She could hardly bear to think of Leroy, of his pale eyes wild with the thoughts he couldn't make words for. "Oh, go away hawk," she called crossly.

The crossness only lasted a few moments for she saw wild strawberries glinting like rubies down among the grasses. Her mouth watered so hard it brought tears to her eyes.

"I didn't know I was so hungry," she murmured as she went down on her knees among the wet grasses and quickly filled her mouth with the sweet sharp-tasting berries. She crawled along picking and eating, her fingers staining bright strawberry red.

"My first perfect out-of-doors breakfast," she gloated after a while, and still on her knees looked at three berries on the palm of her hand. "So tiny. So sharp tasting. So perfect." She paused with her head on one side to listen to the long sweet silence of nature's morning, down the valley, all the way across to the mountains.

"Oh, stop wasting time, Jasmin," she ordered herself sharply, just as her mother would do if she could see her "daydreaming"—what her mother called thinking. "Get up, Jasmin, and go where you're supposed to be going."

She filled her hand with strawberries, then walked on her way, westwards and downwards, nibbling one tiny berry at a time to make them last. "Strawberries for breakfast, strawberries for breakfast," she chanted in rhythm to her hurrying feet, inwardly deciding that once she was settled in her hiding-home that strawberries would be her regular breakfast.

When she'd marched for what seemed a very long time, she came to an edge, a place where the land dropped off almost like a cliff. She must be very near the river. The drop was so sharp that it was difficult to climb down, and made even worse by the pack on her back, and especially by the potato bag in her hand. In places she needed both hands to save herself, as she slipped and slithered grabbing onto branches and roots. It felt as if her potato carrying hand would break. In one place she held the bag in her teeth as she made a daring dive from a stolid tree root to a projecting trunk much lower down. The trees grew sideways out of the earth. Some of them were huge. Everywhere, pale roots, like gnarled ghost fingers clawed out at the air. As she plunged and slid, Jasmin saw that there were dark places like caves under the twisted bodies of some of the giant trees. She shivered, even though her parka made her warm. There was something creepy in the chill shadow of the steep hillside.

Gobs of slimy brown earth clung to her sneakers, making her feet into heavy weights dragging her legs down. No hawk followed her now. Birds and squirrels had gone silent.

Down in the cleft in the earth, the ghostly roots and dark trees made her think of gnomes and evil spells, thoughts she used to think when she was a little kid. There was the dark smell of old mushrooms.

Her hands felt cold, but Jasmin took a deep breath and tried to keep her chin up as she eased her way along the slippery slimy slope, determined that she would not be scared.

After a while of traveling sideways and downwards she came to a break in the hillside, a rugged sort of red-clay gully, jagged and twisted. It was too wide to jump over. Bright water splashed down at the bottom over rocks and pebbles. Carefully she climbed down and caught a drink of ice-cold water in her cupped hand. Looking around, she thought it was like being inside the body of the earth; gray pine-needled skin, then blood-red insides with bulging roots for veins.

"A chip hat had she on." Jasmin tried her voice to see if the sound made her braver. But she wasn't sure. Her voice sounded so little and sharp and lonely, just a weak thing in a strong and powerful space. Unseen ears seemed to be listening. Unknown eyes seemed to be watching. Uneasily, from deep down in the gully, she looked up and all around her, listening for something. There was nothing. Nothing to feel scared about she told herself sharply and

made herself bend and dip into the silvery, icy water for another drink. Just as her hand dipped into the water there was a yelp. A quick thin yelp.

The sudden surprise of the sound made Jasmin's stomach turn a somersault. "Stop it, stop it," she whispered to her thumping heart. She was mad at herself for being so jumpy. "Toughen up," she told herself. She took a deep breath and searched around for the creature that had yelped. The knuckles of her clenched hands were white and strained.

Then, up the opposite slope, she looked right into the yellow eyes and sharp small face of a young coyote. It was just about ten strides up the slope from where she was drinking.

The coyote looked as startled as she felt, as though it had stopped suddenly on its way down to get a drink. Such a little coyote with pricked ears and a shaggy, yellowish coat. Only a poor, shivering, thin little coyote.

As soon as Jasmin moved to straighten up, the coyote darted away, then watched her from higher up the hillside.

A sudden feeling told Jasmin that there was something very interesting about the spot where the coyote had first been standing. A massive jackpine grew thick and sideways out of the earth, then bent upwards at a sharp angle to reach toward the sky. Its heavy bottom branches hung down like a thick, green skirt over some sort of hollow. Maybe it was a hollow where the coyote lived. Maybe its den was behind that heavy curtain of branches. She had to see. As she moved, the coyote stood its ground up the slope, watching her suspiciously. "Don't you worry," she called up to it softly. "I'm only going to investigate. Not going to hurt anything."

She waded through the ice-cold water and scrambled up the slope to the heavily skirted tree. She paused, took a breath for courage, whispered, "Anybody in there?" paused a moment longer then parted the branches and looked behind them. Neat. Oh neato! At about the height of her chest a thick, brownish rock stuck out like a floor in the hillside. It made a wide ledge, and behind it there seemed to be a deep hollow.

Forgetting the coyote, forgetting the gloomy valley and the spooky clawing roots, forgetting everything except the joy of the marvelous discovery, Jasmin took off her pack, her hat, her parka, pushed all her things onto the ledge and hefted herself up. She climbed in through the skirt of branches. Immediately, as soon as she stepped behind the branches, she felt hidden and safe. It was a perfect hiding-home for a fugitive. But, it needed sweeping out. It was scruffy and a bit stinky, with old pine needles, animal hairs and droppings.

"Perfect. Oh perfect!" Jasmin whispered unbelievingly.

The rock ledge was like a balcony with the thick pine branches hanging down like a curtain. The hollow behind went back into the hillside, as though sometime a great hunk of rock had been pushed out

57

to make a little room. It was not very big; not high enough for her to stand in, but with plenty of space for her to sit up, even to kneel up.

She lay down to try it for sleeping size. Just about long enough to stretch out with her toes pointed if she pushed her feet down underneath the rocky wall that jutted out into uneven shelves on the south side.

"And absolutely dry," she rejoiced as she felt around the roof and the walls.

"Coyote, little coyote, you led me to the most perfect place for living in," she murmured with a glance through her green curtain, while she hoped, superstitiously and romantically, that the little coyote had been on the moonlit field with the others last night, and had been watching her ever since on her travels.

"You're crazy, Jasmin." She mocked herself, but liking her story-book thoughts, she stood up on the balcony, looking out through the branches like a princess on her castle wall. "This is the hiding-hollow of Jasmin Marie Antoinette Stalke, wherein she shall dwell—wherein *she shall live as she do please.*

"Shhh," she restrained herself. "Somebody could be looking, listening. Shhhh, nobody is going to find me here. Thank you, coyote."

10

Every time a teacher asked, "And what's Jasmin doing today?" Eglantine made her face dull and answered sullenly, "I don't know." Once Nathaniel Augustus John almost got punished for being rude when he answered, "How should I know what Jasmin's doing?" Merron Damion Hugh, when he was asked, answered, "I ain't never seen her," and was made to write out twenty times in his crooked grade-one letters, "I did not see her this morning." Olive had always warned her children not to talk about family concerns at school. "It's none of their business what we do at home," she said.

But, at two-thirty-five that afternoon, Mr. Jeremy Podluck, the school principal, thought that Jasmin *was* his business. He phoned the Stalke house and let the black phone on the wall ring and ring. "Aw shucks," said Olive. "Why couldn't it wait for a commercial?"

Mr. Jeremy Podluck was patient. At last, when Olive did slip-slop in her pink slippers and pick up the receiver, he said, "Mrs. Stalke, after all our warnings Jasmin is missing school again today."

"Is she now?" said Olive while she tried to think what was the best excuse to make.

"You must know she didn't come to school today, Mrs. Stalke."

"Well, Mr. Podluck, you know how it is round a farm with all these kids. All the jobs to be done." Olive sounded impatient because the exciting moment in the TV hospital serial was just coming up. The wicked nurse was about to pull the plug on the seriously injured beautiful heroine who was the only one who knew the identity of the real killer. While Olive listened to Mr. Podluck she had to keep her eyes and one ear toward the TV.

"Mrs. Stalke, it will be very hard on Jasmin if she fails and doesn't go on into Junior High this year."

"You bet, Mr. Podluck," said Olive and went on to explain cheerfully, "But you see, Mr. Podluck, it'd be really hard on us here if we lost our cattle. This morning, you see, the cattle got out and Jasmin had to get out there and help her dad. So she missed the bus, that's how. See." The young handsome doctor with magnetic blue eyes and crisply curling hair was just coming in behind the wicked nurse. Will he, oh will he be in time? A commercial cut in with a little girl explaining to her rag doll about the softness of toilet tissue.

Mr. Podluck went on, repeating that it's a hard and miserable thing for a child to fail a grade.

Olive laughed shortly and kept her eyes on the TV. "Well, it can't be helped, can it, Mr. Podluck? You can't say as how we ever pretend to be a brainy family, now can you? Jasmin fails, so what? We'll still love her."

"Muv, Muv," the silky headed Carmen Miranda Elisa tugged at her mother's jeans. "Muv, can I have a dolly like that?" She pointed to the TV screen but that commercial had already been replaced by one selling razor blades.

"Sure. Sure thing, Mr. Podluck, I'll make sure she's in school tomorrow. Don't you worry, Mr. Podluck. She'll be in school, that I guarantee. But she's a good girl, you know that, don't you?"

"Mrs. Stalke, we suspect that with a bit of help she could be not only a good girl but a very good student."

"Well, she's a big help to me, with all these children. But, don't worry, Mr. Podluck, I'll see she's in school tomorrow, for sure." She hung up the phone. Any thoughts she had about Jasmin were immediately forgotten. TV was so exciting. Good, oh good, the handsome doctor was going to save the beautiful patient. Then Leroy sprang up, wide awake from his long troubled sleep. He sprang up over the top of Honey Angelina who was on the floor banging a carrot on a tin pan while she gurgled at the pictures flicking across the TV. The baby yelled. Olive picked up the baby and sent Carmen Miranda Elisa up the ladder to find some clothes for Leroy who was still in his underwear.

"Hush now. Hush now," Olive crooned calmly to her troublesome children. Then, with Honey Angelina on her knee and her eyes on the handsome doctor who was going to fall in love with the beautiful patient, she half helped Leroy to get himself dressed. "You are the funny one," she teased him.

"It's real hot outside and you want to put on this big thick jacket. Silly Leroy. Don't be silly. Be a good boy."

Leroy got angry. He pushed his mother away and tugged the thick red and blue plaid jacket away from her. Then, with fierce shaking of his head and argumentative noises, he pushed his arms into the sleeves and struggled to do up the buttons with his thick strong fingers.

"Silly boy. See now you're hiding the pretty horsy on your T-shirt." Olive humored him as he did up the last button covering up the words CAL-GARY STAMPEDE. "I thought you liked the pretty T-shirt Jassy buyed you."

Leroy stopped still with his hands on the front of his thick jacket and stared at his mother, the baby, and pretty pale-headed Carmen Miranda Elisa. He looked as though a big thought was happening in his mind but he only made a grunt and folded his arms as though to say defiantly, "I've decided to wear this jacket and nobody will stop me."

"Okay, Leroy." Olive smiled and kissed him quickly on the cheek. "You wear it. Anything for a quiet life. But don't come round me when you're dying of heat stroke. I've got just too many things on my mind to want any more trouble."

She did have a lot of things on her mind. There must be miles of fence down to be keeping Bud busy with it all day. He'd kept saying they needed money to buy new fence posts and wire. Where was the money to come from? Always something needing money on a farm. And she was mad at Bud anyhow. He was getting too handy at keeping Jasmin out to help him. Doing it too often. Didn't he know that Jasmin was needed round the house?

"I do hope that girl's back in the house to help me make supper," she cooed to the baby. "We need our Jassy here, don't we? Jassy does a nice job with cooking, don't she? And I got to make the pie, nice blueberry pie I promised 'em all. Nice lot o' juicy big berries they all picked yesterday before Nathaniel and Leroy, bless him, played their Tarzan game. Doesn't look to me like our Jassy is going to be here to make herself useful in time, does it, my Honey Angelina, lovey?"

Eventually though, Olive really had to get started on getting supper ready for when the kids got home from school. "Lovey, love," she said to Leroy soothingly, "you go out and pump up two nice buckets of nice fresh water for Momma." She put the buckets in his hands and pointed him toward the back door, murmuring baby words to him, "Nice, nice, Leroy get nice water for Momma. Nice Leroy."

It was lovely that the handsome doctor was going to fall in love with the beautiful patient who knew the identity of the real killer. It was so lovely that Olive sat down again on the edge of the chesterfield cuddling Honey Angelina and dreaming her television dreams, and Carmen Miranda Elisa snuggled her pale head against her soft mother.

Outside, Leroy lifted his eyes to the hot afternoon sun and searched for his mind. Then, while he slowly and gradually found his memories, he worked the long creaking handle of the pump, up, down-up, down-up, down. He made a slow rhythm and laughed gleefully when the bright water gushed and dinned into the tin bucket. He laughed at every rush of gleaming water that his strong arms pumped up out of the earth.

When both buckets were brimming full and spilling little sparkling rivulets, Marigold Lolita May, the wild one with the laughing dirty face, climbed down off the old tractor she had been pretending to drive while the others stayed indoors. She was smudged and streaked from head to toe with black grease and brown rust. She ran to be with Leroy. She ran under the jetting gleaming water, gasping and screaming at the icy cold. Leroy went on pumping harder and faster till the pump was creaking, and he opened his mouth and laughed out loud for joy as his dirty, dark little sister pranced and danced in and out of the spray, dripping and splashing.

Then suddenly, the game was over. Leroy easily picked up one brimming bucket in each strong hand and hefted the heavy weight of water into the house. He carefully set the two buckets under the wash table by the front door, using his strength to keep the buckets level without spilling.

But Marigold Lolita May didn't care a thing about spilling on the floor. Mischievous and laughing she danced in after Leroy, spraying water from her hair and dripping clothes like a wet dog shaking itself. She was making lakes and rivers all over the gray linoleum.

Olive jumped up, forgetting the TV show. "Well! Well!" she burst out. "Just look what you're doing." She ran, puffing, at the little girl. Marigold Lolita May dodged behind the chesterfield, then behind the table, teasing and tantalising.

And while the chase was on, Leroy slipped out into the sunshine. His mind was clear. He had found his memories. He hurried in his rolling, lurching way past the rusting cars and machinery out onto the road. But this time he didn't walk on the road where he might be seen. This time he walked down in the deep roadside ditch where the feathery summer grasses were lush and tall and tickly. His fingertips touched the faces of lanky brown-eyed daisies. His knees sent sweet pollen rising from wide, white, starry flowerheads of yarrow. He tried not to break the pretty flowers or to tread on the wild, earth-smelling mushrooms. If they broke round his feet the hurt mushrooms looked at him darkly with their broken black undersides and made him sorry. Sorry, sorry, sorry, he tried to say to flowers and butterflies and mushrooms and bending grasses as he trod and pushed his way through them. Sorry, sorry, sorry for Jasmin. He heard her crying. Poor Jasmin. He had to tell her, sorry for breaking her pretty plants. Jasmin never cried. Nobody made Jasmin cry. He had done it. He had made his sister cry. He had to find her and make her better.

When he heard the roar and crunch of the

65

school bus that would have already let off Eglantine, Nathaniel and little Merron Damion, he put his bright, white head down among the cool, smooth-smelling mushrooms because he knew that his hair shone and told people where he was. But when the van had gone by and all was safe, Leroy lurched on westwards and downwards, westwards and downwards, in the deep summer-scented ditch with his arms flailing like storm-driven windmills. His strange broken voice kept trying to call, "Jasmin. Jasmin."

11

In a burst of joyful energy, Jasmin swept out her new home with a leafy broken bough for a broom, all the time keeping an ear listening to the outside sounds.

Swish of the broom, gurgle of water—but no sound of disturbed squirrels or birds.

"Safe. I'll know I'm safe when nothing is rousing my wilderness," she told herself, repeating, "my wilderness," with a smile of delicious satisfaction. "My own wilderness."

When she peeked out through her curtain the coyote looked back into her eyes from a watching place a few yards down the hill. "Hi," she called softly. "You be my watchdog. If you run away, I'll know there's danger, and I'll dive into my hiding-hollow, safe—never to be found."

As she swept off and polished the rough shelves on her south wall her thoughts slipped hither and thither, from the lovely present to the worries of the past. "But why won't past worries stay in the past?" she fretted as Leroy and all the family troubles nagged at her happiness. "Eglantine can take my place," she told herself firmly and worked all the harder cleaning and organizing. She wanted her den to be the most beautiful place she had ever dreamed of.

Sometimes in the Stalke house she had tried putting a jar of wild flowers on the table but they had got mixed up with the bread and bits of food, or the little kids had knocked them over, or her mother had said, "Oh Jasmin, this ain't the place for your fancy ideas." So, in her own home, as soon as it was all swept out, Jasmin put a bunch of tiny violets where they looked nice on a red rock shelf. She found them growing in a mossy patch just above her place, up the hillside. She made a solid pot to put them in out of some of the gucky earth that stuck to her sneakers. While the outside dried quickly until it felt like cool leather, the inside stayed wet enough to keep the stems moist. The gucky stuff, she found out as she pushed and rolled it in her hands, was clay. Real red clay. Ideas bounced in her mind. With clay she could make herself dishes and pots and bowls. She decided she would start on that when she had everything organised and was well settled in.

On the shelves, against the bright violets, she

propped up her soft leather-bound book so the gold edges showed, a bit glittery even in the shadowy place. She hung out her quilt to dry and her red gown to let the creases shake out of it. As she worked the sun moved round in the sky until it was shining on her side of the deep valley.

The job that took the longest was collecting enough pine needles to make a soft bed. She had decided to lay them down thickly in the hollow behind her balcony to make a mattress. That took ages. She used the plastic potato sack, filling it up again and again, then emptying it carefully exactly where she wanted the mattress. When the quilt was dry she spread it over the pine-needle bed. It looked cosy; a bright couch. At night she could lie on one half of the quilt and fold the other half over, like a sleeping bag. She rolled her parka up to make a pillow, then lay down for a few minutes to enjoy it all. It felt green and secret in there, sun dappling in through the pine-branch drapes and the scent of the earth mixing with pine needles and violets.

Common sense told her that she mustn't keep food in her hiding home unless she wanted to have bears for company, which she didn't. So, she built an arrangement with flat rocks down in the gully in the ice cold rivulet, a refrigerator and a larder combined. There she put her five remaining potatoes and a few large mushrooms she had already found. She knew quite a lot about mushrooms, which ones were good to eat and which were bad for the stomach. The Stalke family used wild mushrooms all summer, and every child had been taught about the few poisonous ones as soon as they could walk.

Jasmin did think that she would like to make friends with the little coyote that kept watching her from a distance. Ever since she could remember she had longed for a dog. She had imagined herself and Leroy running across the fields with a dog prancing beside them. She'd imagined putting her hand out of bed to feel the rough coat of a dog who would be her friend. She could put her head on it when she felt miserable. But whenever she'd asked her father if she could have a dog he'd yelled that there were enough mouths to feed without them getting pets. Perhaps the coyote could become her first pet.

As soon as her work was done she tried to edge nearer the coyote. It only darted away and watched her from farther up the hill. Patiently she tried again and again, whispering to it, calling it Missy, for it seemed female. The poor timid shivering thing listened to her and tried to stand still but always at the last moment, as she almost got near, it snapped is sharp teeth and ran away. Even so, Jasmin was excited. She thought she would tame it in the end.

The sun got very hot and as it dried up her side of the valley it brought up from the earth all sorts of wild scents. Jasmin pulled her straw hat down to shade her eyes and sat below her balcony catching the haunting fragrances of the forest—pines and fresh leaves, tree saps, warm moss, musky deer. There was even the dry straw smell of her own hat, her chip hat, *a chip hat had she on.*

When all the work was done the day began to go slowly. Jasmin wasn't going to risk moving far away from her hiding place to get more food yet. She thought she had enough for a while. There was no use taking risks and being found by searchers. Really she would have liked to have gone back to the open place to find more strawberries. But that was too risky. She rolled her jeans up and spread herself out in the sunshine. It was so strange to be by herself. No baby to carry. No Leroy. Nobody to look after. Just herself. She couldn't remember ever being by herself before. It was nice. Peaceful. But time began to go slowly. So slowly.

She wished she dared go to find the river. Her ears were getting so tuned to the wilderness noises that she thought she could hear the swishing of flowing water way through the trees. Her ears were getting sharper all the time. She could hear the hiss and tinkle, the laps and gurgles of the rivulet waters round rocks and pebbles in her gully. She could hear the buzz of afternoon insects, the whispering of their filmy wings.

She decided she'd better not waste time just sitting. She ought to start making her dishes. If she got enough clay to make a dish it would be dry and ready for when it was safe to go out and collect strawberries.

With the coyote always moving around and watching her from a distance, Jasmin climbed up the hillside above her den and found a broken place where the layer of clay was exposed under the thin piney gray soil. She knew all about that acid gray soil from her science project. Was it only yesterday that her project had been ruined? It seemed ages ago. What a lot had happened since then.

Using a sharp flat stone for cutting into the surface, and her fingers for digging, she managed to get some hunks of damp brown clay and push them together in the ever-useful plastic sack. It was very heavy, loaded with clay, when she hauled it up onto her balcony. The afternoon was hot.

She rested in the green shade on her balcony, breaking off a handful of clay which she began to play with thoughtfully. She liked the feel of clay and she went over in her mind all the things the teacher had taught them when they made ashtrays at school. She had made a terrible ashtray. When she took it home her mother had said, "We've got enough junk without school sending home stuff like that. I don't know why they don't teach you something useful."

Funny, she could remember such a lot about school now she had thinking time. She remembered that you had to knead the clay to drive out all the air bubbles and that you had to keep it warm to make it pliable. She kneaded the clay on the warm thigh of her jeans, not caring about the big brown stain it was making. She kneaded it for a long thoughtful time until it was beautifully smooth, warm and easy to shape, a smooth silkiness in her fingers. It hadn't been fun making an ashtray. Her mother was right! Hers had been thick and clumsy, an ugly thing. She supposed she just hadn't cared much about making an ashtray.

Warm on the leafy balcony, Jasmin felt her fingers loving the silky clay and making a happiness in her mind. She began to hum softly. Her fingers were pushing and pulling and smoothing as though they had found a life of their own. When she was little she had watched her grandmother's fingers make a needle flash through bright bits of cloth, as garments for a new baby grew in her hands. Now her own clumsy fingers were going to make a bowl. That's what she was telling them to make. The fingers of one hand dug themselves inside her warm ball of clay while the fingers of the other hand began pushing and pulling delicately and firmly. Somehow, they didn't feel like her normal clumsy fingers. They began to work as if they knew exactly what to do. They weren't making a bowl at all; they were making a spiky porcupine. The clay porcupine began to grow as if by a sort of magic and Jasmin's mind began to work with her fingers. She became completely absorbed, forgetting her troubles and dangers. She forgot everything except the clay in her fingers and the problem of putting into it the happy feeling of the amber porcupine she had seen in the morning sunshine at her first waking in the wilderness.

It wasn't easy. It was a problem to keep the spines sharp and delicate. It was tricky and fiddly to fashion the sad little face. But, slowly and carefully, the porcupine took a fragile shape in her hands. It was so hard not to squash one set of spines while she was sharpening the ones on the other side. But she did it, and she was surprised and delighted. She had no idea she could make such a thing. It was much better than that terrible ashtray. The porcupine had a happy feeling to it. Maybe it wasn't perfect but she liked it. She liked it a lot. In fact, she thought it was a miracle.

What was more, while she had been making it time had gone quickly. She had been so absorbed that her worries had been pushed clean out of her head. She thought she would like to make something else right away—just to see if she could. Maybe it was just an accident. After all, a porcupine is a pretty easy thing to make. Even a little kid could make a porcupine. Uncertainty teeter-tottered with the pleasure she felt in the porcupine. Was it really a clever thing? Could her fingers make something else? Could they find that same skill again?

12

BACK AT THE STALKE HOME THE KIDS RUSHED IN OFF the school bus past the junk of cars and machinery, scattering the bright bantam hens. They dumped their lunch pails and homework books on the floury table where Olive was up to her elbows in making pastry for the blueberry pie.

"Hey, listen here, youse guys," she warned them before any other word could be spoken, "remember what you have to do." She pointed a floury

73

finger toward the ladder. "Remember what I told you this morning. You'd best have it all cleaned out up there before your Dad gets in—or else!"

Nathaniel gave her a cheeky look out of his laughing face. "He won't care," he sang out. "Dad's in the beer parlor in Dandron."

"Yes," Merron Damion Hugh supported his big brother, all the time looking at his mother with big serious eyes. "We seen Dad's truck outside the beer parlor when the bus comed past."

"Aw shucks, wouldn't you know it! Just one more thing." Olive sighed. "Did any of youse see Jasmin?"

"No," Eglantine and Nathaniel said together.

"She's gonna be in big trouble at school," Nathaniel chirped, hoping his mother would forget about the mess up in the attic.

"Never mind about school!" Olive exploded. "She's going to be in real trouble here if she don't show up to help me soon. I ain't set eyes on that girl all day."

"You mean she's just played hookey and had a holiday all day! Serves her right she's going to fail her grade!" Eglantine said with her eyes flashing. "She should have cleaned up the things upstairs. You should have made her, Mom."

"How could I have made her when I never got to see her?" said Olive. "Anyhow, it's youse guys I'm going to make clean it up, up there. Go on." She pushed them all toward the ladder, fussy like a fat hen, clucking, "Go on, up you go, all of youse."

Olive's floury handmarks were on them all as they scrambled grumbling up the ladder.

"So, he's in the beer parlor, is he," she cooed to Honey Angelina who was propped up in her baby seat among the cooking things, lunch pails and home-work books. "If he's in the beer parlor, what's he left Jasmin doing?" Honey Angelina gurgled, trying to focus her eyes on the flour cloud as Olive lifted her hands high to let air sift into the fine mixture to make her pastry light.

"That man o' mine had better learn right off that I won't have him keeping Jasmin out of the house when I need her. That's right, isn't it? my Honey Angelina, isn't it then? That Dad's got to learn that we need our Jasmin, hasn't he then?" She popped a juicy, fat blueberry into the baby's mouth. Honey Angelina pushed it out with her tongue and started to cry.

"Oh, my messy girl," Olive cooed, picking the baby up with her floury hands, holding her up to the ceiling, dancing her around—and immediately forgetting all about Jasmin.

Upstairs, Eglantine, Nathaniel, Merron, Carmen, and Marigold grumblingly pulled their beds straight and stuffed their possessions under beds and pillows.

"You do Leroy's and Jasmin's or I'll tell Mom you've broke your glasses," Nathaniel blackmailed Eglantine.

"Telltale—you!" Eglantine hissed at him but went over to sort out Leroy's bedding. She looked

75

down the side of Jasmin's bed and underneath it for the patchwork quilt. "Jasmin's problem," she muttered to herself. "See if I care if Leroy's thrown it out the window or some other stupid thing. Oh, you little nuisance," she fumed because Marigold was pulling Carmen's bed apart as fast as Carmen tried to put it together. "Do you think I've got nothing better to do than look after a bunch of little kids?" Eglantine scolded them all as she yanked the covers on the littlest ones' beds.

"I wish Jasmin was here," Carmen whimpered.

"She's out playing with Leroy, as usual. Getting out of work because of poor Leroy. Poor Leroy," Eglantine went on sarcastically, kicking things under the beds.

Pretty soon, Bud got home with his hat on the back of his head, his knees a bit wobbly, and one eye he had to struggle to keep open.

"Where's my supper, Woman," he called out again and again in a beer-slurred voice, pretending he was happy as a king.

It was only when they were all about to sit down that Olive shouted over the television, "Hey, where's Leroy?"

She looked around for anybody to answer her. "He was here a bit ago when I started to make supper. Anybody seen him?"

"He pumped water and made me all wet," Marigold Lolita May told them, sucking in her cheeks as she looked at her mother.

"I'll give him Leroy!" Bud waved an arm threateningly and his hat fell forward over his face as he lurched backwards on his chair. Screams of laughter roared out of the TV.

"Ain't seen him since we comed home," Nathaniel shouted over the din, "nor Jasmin neither, we ain't seen, have we?" He looked around for confirmation from all the others but they were too busy trying to dig into their hamburgers without missing any of the action on TV.

"Oh well." Olive sighed, relaxing heavily into her chair. "One thing we know for sure, Leroy will be where Jasmin is. Hey Bud." She prodded him. He pushed his hat up off his face, looked confusedly at his supper and picked up his fork. Then he let it fall out of his hand as he slipped back in his chair again.

"Oh"—Olive shook her head resignedly—"no good trying to talk to you while you're in this state. Makes me wonder why I ever bothered to slave to make this nice supper for you. You keeping Jasmin out, an' all, so I had to do it all by myself. It's hard without Jasmin, you know, hard on me."

"Huh!" was all Bud said, then began to snore.

Eglantine flashed her eyes. "You think Jasmin's perfect. Well, I think I know something about her," she said spitefully.

"I don't think you can know anything bad about our Jasmin, so don't come that," Olive reprimanded Eglantine, which only made her want all the more to say something awful.

"I bet she's run away," Eglantine burst out.

"Don't be silly. Jasmin wouldn't do a thing like that. She's never done a thing to worry us in her life.

She's just off wandering somewhere, keeping Leroy happy," Olive said confidently as she popped mashed-up food from her plate into Honey Angelina's mouth.

"I double bet she's run away," Eglantine persisted, shouting over TV.

"Shh," her mother hissed frowning at the picture and tilting her head to catch the words.

Exasperated, Eglantine shouted all the louder. "If you don't believe me, go upstairs and look. She's taken her quilt. And her parka's gone from under her bed." Suddenly Eglantine believed what she was saying. "She's run away because she's in trouble at school, see."

Olive looked less certain. She prodded Bud again. "Bud, Bud, are you listening to what Eglantine's trying to tell us?"

Bud groaned. Olive put her face near to his and speaking slowly and very loud tried to get his attention. "Do you hear? She says Jasmin's run away. Must have gone after you finished getting the cattle back in. Bud, Eglantine say's Jasmin's run away. Leroy's gone with her. Do you hear, Bud? Jasmin and Leroy have run away."

For a minute, because there was only a commercial on, all the faces round the table stared to see what Bud would do.

His head swayed. One eye opened. He pushed his hat back. A faraway smile slipped over his face and his words slurred out slowly. "Isht fun to run away. I ushed to run away." He laughed drunkenly. "You bet. I ushed to run away, run away, away, a-waay." He drifted away into his memory with both his eyes closed, then suddenly said, almost soberly, "They'll come back, come running back soon as they're good an' hungry—and cold, cold. I remember —cold—cold. Noshing to worry about. They'll come running home when they're hungry and cold— cold—" His head dropped forward on his chest and he sank back into his snoring sleep.

"Well, even if they have run away, I guess he's right. Bet they'll be back soon as it gets dark—whatever. Come on, the rest of youse, get on now and clean up your plates," Olive said.

That was that for the time being.

Eglantine and Nathaniel had the pieces of blueberry pie that should have been for Leroy and Jasmin. "Serves her right," gloated Eglantine, licking her lips.

Marigold scraped out the pie dish ending up with blue stains all round her mouth. Everybody teased her. Nobody bothered to clear away the dirty dishes from the table because that was Jasmin's job. They all settled down to watch exciting adventures on TV—except Bud. He just snored.

It went on like that in the Stalke house until the sun was dipping red behind the purple mountains.

13

JASMIN SAT ON HER BALCONY WATCHING THE COYOTE. It had settled in a shallow hollow while she had been quietly working her clay. It was curled, nose under tail, in a patch of shade down the hillside, its eyes ever watchful of the girl on the balcony and its ears ever twitching. My watchdog, thought Jasmin.

That was what she would try to make next. Curled like that, the coyote would be a perfect model for the new ball of clay she had made ready by slowly kneading it in the hot sunshine on her thigh. When it was smooth and pliant she had kept it warm in her hands, turning it and turning it until the idea of what to make came to her.

She watched the coyote through the curtain of her pine branches and her fingers began to press and push the clay to make the curve of its body, the thin sides, the line of the backbone, the sharp pointed face and the half-pricked twitching ears. It was slow work. This time as she worked with her fingers her mind was asking questions. Why was the coyote puppy by itself? Where were its parents? It looked like a sad and deserted little thing. Jasmin bit her lip to remember her father's coyote traps in the thick, marshy grass at the end of one pasture. She had seen coyotes caught in those traps by a foot or a leg. She'd seen them struggling to get free until her father went with his gun and shot them. That was a thing she hated. Her father said he had to trap them because they were cattle killers and because they stole the chickens. He said that, thought Jasmin. But she couldn't ever remember a calf being killed. Once she had seen a coyote get away with one of her mother's hens in its mouth. When her father shot a coyote he hung the carcass on a tree behind the outhouse, up by the hind legs, then he slit it down its belly and pulled the bloody body out of the skin. He threw the body to the pigs in the pen and sold the skins for good money.

Jasmin always hated that part of the farm. As her fingers worked to turn the clay in her hand into a coyote pup she breathed uneasily remembering the frightened eyes of coyotes in her father's traps. She wondered if the frightened feeling would go down her fingers and into the shaggy little curved body she was making.

It was long and delicate work to make the texture of the shaggy rough fur. She tried using bits of pine needle and sharp twig to prick the clay with. It took ages to find the exact right pointy twig to make the tiny openings for the watchful eyes. She almost had to hold her breath to keep her hand steady for such exacting hollows. Yes, she thought, yes, she was making another fairly good thing. She really did have some skill in her fingers. If she was honest, she thought her two animals were marvelous. She kept looking at the porcupine and the coyote and turning them round. Already the points of the porcupine spines were beginning to dry and go paler. She moistened each spine carefully with her tongue remembering from school that clay left to dry too quickly cracks and breaks. Crazy what a lot she remembered about lessons from school now she had got away from it! She remembered that clay has to be dried slowly. Another use for her useful plastic bag. She placed the small porcupine and the curled coyote in the bag, making a sort of plastic room. Because there was nobody to see her behave like a little kid, she lay on her stomach and put her head down against the opening of the plastic room and looked in on the animals she had made, like looking into a magic world. The folds of the plastic with the sun shining through were like hills and valleys and ravines in a shining landscape. And her animals looked perfect in there.

"Why didn't I know I could do it?" she whispered, awed by the skill she had found in her fingers, remembering that ever since she had been a little kid trying her very best the teachers had got mad at her because she couldn't color in between the lines of the pictures they duplicated. She had always known she was just a messy failure. But looking in on her two animals she felt pretty successful and her imagination began going wild, telling her she could make a forest in there by sticking bits of boughs in clay. She could make more animals. The bear? Could she remember enough to make the bear? Why hadn't she found out about the cleverness in her fingers before? If only she had known she could do it, she could have made things for the little kids to play with. She suddenly thought of them all; fluffy Carmen Miranda Elisa, wild Marigold Lolita May, timid Merron Damion Hugh, chubby Nathaniel. Perhaps Leroy would find that he had clever fingers and would make things for the kids now that Jasmin didn't live with them. A lump rose in her throat and tears smarted in her eyes. Maybe they were all out searching for her at that very moment, calling her name across the road and the fields. She listened but she couldn't hear anybody calling.

She rested her cheek on her arm remembering all her family. Maybe Eglantine was already glad that Jasmin had run away. Now she could be the oldest and have the bed by the window. Leroy didn't count. Poor Leroy. Her mother had those blueberries to make a pie for supper. Jasmin's mouth watered. Her stomach said it was hungry. Perhaps it would be okay to take a risk, to make a dash up the hill and dine on strawberries.

She decided it might be all right. She parted the branches and was about to climb down from her balcony when she noticed that the coyote was not there. Somewhere a squirrel was chattering madly. A fat bumblebee was humming loudly. She fell back on her bed with her heart beating like thunder in her ears. Whatever was happening?

Out there an engine had roared into action, thumpathumpa thumpathumpthumthum. The engine died. Silence, except for her heart in her ears.

Thoughts shuddered through Jasmin's stunned mind. That was an engine. A small engine. Somebody was trying to start a small engine, like one on a trailbike. It must be a junior high school boy out looking for her on his trailbike.

It started again. Thumpathumpthumpthump, then, thum—thum, blasting the air, echoing in the sky.

She flattened herself down, pushing her mouth onto her quilt, the pine needles whispering in her mattress. Oh no! No junior high school boy must find her. Suppose it was Doug Mason. She used to have daydreams about him, that they were in a TV commercial together running hand in hand in slow motion, her brown hair floating and his black hair shining in the sunlight. She hadn't brought a comb. She must look like a wild scarecrow by now. But, nobody, nobody was going to find her. She pressed herself down harder into her mattress.

The engine died away. Then it started again.

What a joke, a junior high boy out looking for her. Some joke. No boy would want to look for Jasmin Marie Antoinette Stalke. They all knew she was just an ugly dummy Stalke kid.

Again the engine roared out its noise. Then it died. She could hardly breathe. She tried to stop her heart from beating. There were footsteps on the pine needles. Crunching footsteps.

She thought her head and chest would burst. The footfalls continued steadily. She couldn't stand it any longer. She had to know what was out there. So, cautiously, she eased herself along on her stomach until she was on her balcony and could just see out. She didn't believe it. Those heavy footfalls belonged to a fat spruce grouse. Well! That was crazy!

But what about the engine? The spruce grouse couldn't be the one riding a trailbike.

There it was again. Thumpathumpthumpa-thumthumthum—the engine seemed to be right underneath her balcony. While the engine was still thumping she took a big breath and hung over the edge to peer down below the tufts of green pine needles.

She burst out laughing. She rolled back on her bed, kicked up her legs and nearly died of laughing. Some engine. Some trailbike. Some junior high school boy! It was only the male grouse. His tail was lifted behind him like a brilliantly patterned fan, reds and browns and white. And the thumping of the engine was only that same grouse violently beating his wings, thumping his wings to call a lady grouse. That was all. Crazily, Jasmin kicked her feet up into the air and laughed at her silly mistake. Silly Jasmin Marie Antoinette silly Stalke thinking a junior high school boy would be out looking for her. "You're crazy," she said aloud to herself. But anyhow, it's just like a junior high school boy showing off like they do."

Then suddenly, while she was still laughing, there was a terrible commotion outside; a squawking and a squalling. She jumped up in horror and looked out in time to see the swift snap of the little coyote's jaws on the neck of the proud puffed grouse. Those beautiful feathers were suddenly nothing more than a drooping heap being carried away into the bushes in the coyote's trap of a mouth. Now Jasmin's heart was thumping again, thumping quickly like the trailbike engine. She looked down where a few fluffy feathers clung and trembled on the forest floor in a smear of blood. She shuddered. Her pet coyote was a tough killer. Still, she had to remember that wild things had to kill to survive. Maybe she would have to kill to survive. Could she?

Serious thoughts filled her mind and her uneasy fears made her shiver as she heard the far and near sounds of the wilderness and saw that the hot afternoon was turning into insect-buzzing evening. The rivulet down in the deep gorge whispered like a ghost thing. Her stomach rumbled with hunger.

14

LEROY STOPPED. HE STOPPED AS IF HE WAS LISTENING, his arms spread like wings, his mouth open, his head to one side, among the dandelion clocks and grasses in the ditch. The cloud of mosquitoes following him down the winding downward roadside stopped with him, like a buzzing golden mist around his white head. Leroy was smiling. With his fingers spread wide, he glided his arms forward, then back, back, then forward. He laughed because he felt small breezes swimming under and over his fingers. He was making cool breezes round his hands, making cool breezes in the hot air. Happily, he went on walking again gliding his arms forward and back,

back and forward, enjoying the sensation that had filled his mind and made him forget to call Jasmin. Suddenly he remembered to call her again to tell her he was there.

Inside his thick plaid jacket it was hot like being in the bathtub. Swish, swish his rubber boots swished together like a cow's tail swishing flies in long grass. Leroy swished a big butterfly up out of the grasses and watched it dance on a dandelion, a dandelion with a face like the sun. "Don't look at the sun, Leroy; it will make your eyes water." He heard Jasmin say that. He could hear Jasmin talking in his head even though she had gone away because he had hurt her pretty plants. In his head he heard her crying. He heard her say again, "Don't look at the sun, Leroy. Your pale eyes can't stand it." Because he could hear Jasmin in his head telling him, he closed his eyes, but it was too late. He had been in the bright sun too long. He felt hot tears squeezing out of his eyes and he tried to call for Jasmin again. He put out his hand for her to lead him and she wouldn't take it. But in the dark inside his head he could see Jasmin kneeling down among the grass stalks for the strong, cool leaves of a healing plant.

Leroy watched in his head for the pictures and he knelt down among the grass stalks and dandelions and he felt around, crawling forward, until he found cool, wide leaves, then he broke them off and put one on each eye as Jasmin would for him. In his head he could hear her telling him to put himself down in the shade and have a little sleep until his eyes felt better. She would sit with her arms round her knees watching the butterflies and wait for him. He went to sleep smiling because in his head he could see her watching and she wasn't crying anymore. He slept for a long time.

When he woke he was shivery. His eyes were better but Jasmin had gone. The mosquitoes had bitten his hands and face. The sun had gone and the night was coming cool. He hurt where the mosquitoes had fed on him and he began to rub the places. Then he heard Jasmin in his head again. She said, "Don't scratch, Leroy." Then he heard her crying again. He remembered he had hurt her plants and made her cry. There, he heard a little cry again at the top of the ditch on the field side.

Leroy forgot about shivering and hurting. The crying filled his mind, calling him to climb up the ditch and find it. It was coming from down in the long grass on the other side of the fence.

Leroy squirmed along on his stomach until the pitiful cries were under his chin. Then with his big hands he parted the grasses and saw a kitten with its paw caught in the teeth of an old trap. He made soothing noises in his throat as he tried to calm the terrified creature. Gently he stroked it until he could spread a hand over it and hold it still. Then, remembering the way his father did it, he forced open the tight jaw of the trap and eased the small paw out. He rubbed it between his fingers to bring back life, but only for a moment because the kitten yowled wildly and twisted itself out of his hands. A low growllike cry answered and a massive black cat surged through the grass stalks, picked the kitten up by the head, and sprang away with the small body swinging limply.

Leroy laughed, sitting up in the grasses, rubbing his hands as he watched the mother cat disappear with her kitten.

The crying had stopped. His hands were wet with the night dew and his legs were wet through his jeans. Leroy shivered. He looked all around him and shook his head to try to get his thoughts in order. The crying was gone. The cat had taken it away to the mountains. The mountains were black. The sun had gone. The sun had gone where Jasmin was. Jasmin.

"Jasmin." Dark sounds called out of his mouth, noises that he thought cried, "Jasmin." Leroy began to run with his rubber boots sloshing, following the way the cats had gone, running clumsily where the sun had gone, toward the place where Jasmin had gone.

15

"CAN'T WE STAY UP TILL JASMIN AND LEROY COME home?" the kids begged every time Olive tried to drive them up to bed.

When Bud gasped and snorted as though he was about to wake up, Olive put her finger to her lips to warn everybody to leave him alone. "He won't be in any mood for coping with youse guys," she warned them and managed finally to shoo them all up the ladder, but not before Honey Angelina was screaming with a bad attack of colic. "One thing after another," Olive moaned tiredly as she walked round and round the room with the baby on her shoulder rubbing its back.

"I'll give 'em Tarzan," was the first thing Bud cried out in the confusion of waking and, "Shucks, Olive, can't you keep that baby quiet?"

"They haven't come home, do'ye hear me? I'm worried out o' my mind while you do nothing but snore. Remember, Leroy and Jasmin. They haven't come home. I'm going to lay down with the baby, see if I can get her off. You'd best do something about them two out there."

"Ugh." Bud stretched. So he hadn't been dreaming. Those kids had taken off. "They'll be back," he muttered thickly after Olive as she went into the other room with the screaming baby. He poured himself a cup of coffee to wake himself up and when a commercial came on went to the door to listen outside. "Maybe I should saddle up old Sam, get out and round them kids up," he said to the starry sky. "No. Let 'em get cold and hungry, do 'em good," he argued with himself. "But what if Leroy has one of his attacks? Guess I oughta get out there." "No. It'll be good experience. Let him learn the hard way—and her."

Olive dozed, then woke up with a start remembering something was wrong. Her arm had gone to sleep under Honey Angelina and she hardly dared move in case of waking the baby. She called in a squeaky whisper into a quiet bit of TV, "Bud, Bud, any sign of them kids yet?"

Bud went to the bedroom door. "You calling?" he whispered.

"Bud, them kids back yet? Shh—don't wake the baby."

"Nope. No sign."

"Shh. It must be two in the morning. Bud, you said they'd come home," Olive whispered plaintively.

Bud grunted and lit up a cigarette, the sudden flame of the match in the dark room making Honey Angelina throw up her hands and cry out in a spasm. "Shhh. Shhh," Olive murmured. "But Bud, just listen to them coyotes, will you. Shhh, Honey, shhhh."

"Don't worry," Bud whispered and got out of the room before the baby woke, muttering to himself, "Ain't nothing to worry about. Them coyotes got a kill, carcass of something. Suppose I'd better get out and see. But most likely nothing to worry about. That Jasmin's got enough brains for the two of them. Most likely she packed up some grub to keep 'em going a while. Better take a flashlight with me." He picked one up from the top of the refrigerator and went out leaving the late night movie talking to itself.

Eglantine wasn't asleep. She lay looking across the two empty beds to the moon at the window and listening to the ghastly screaming of the coyotes. She shivered at the bloodcurdling noises in the wilderness but breathed almost silent words angrily into her blanket. "Serves her right. Serves her right. Why should I be left to do all the work?" Then she heard something under the window and sat up in bed. She thought she heard Leroy grunting.

Noiselessly, careful not to wake the sleeping children, she crept to Jasmin's bed, standing on it to peer out. A long shadowy shape was crossing the farm yard, shining a flashlight into dark places; into the black cave of the outhouse, into the shadows behind the henhouse illuminating soft piles of yellow straw, into the big old barn. It was only her father. She heard his voice like a ghost in the emptiness calling, "Jasmin, are you there? Jasmin."

"Jasmin! His precious Jasmin. So, he's worried now, is he?" Eglantine let the words breathe out of her. She almost jumped out of her skin when a body touched her shoulder and stood against her. "Nathaniel," she hissed then caught her breath to threaten, "Wake the kids up—you, and I'll kill you. Shh."

Nathaniel shivered. He was only wearing his skimpy shorts. He leaned his head toward the shadowy figure of his father while whispering sarcastically, "He said they'd come home when it was dark and they was good and hungry, didn't he, Eg?"

"He don't know everything," Eglantine said shortly.

Silently, they both watched as their father moved over to the horse barn then came out again with a saddle across his arm.

Nathaniel nudged Eglantine. "He must be real worried. He's going to ride out and look for them."

"His precious Jasmin." Eglantine sniffed. "Why should she have all the fun?" Then she had an idea, pushed her glasses up her nose and said close to Nathaniel's ear urgently, "Let's you and me go find her, go find them. You and me by ourselves. Sneak out."

"Yeah. Watch which way Dad takes off for. Make sure he doesn't see us. Yeah, oh yeah." Nathaniel was enthusiastic.

Soon, when Eglantine had made sure the TV was only talking to itself, the two of them crept down the ladder, quickly across the *for everything room* and out into the night to dash like crooks on TV, bent and dodging from shadow to shadow among the upturned cars until they found a good place to hide where they could catch their breath and listen.

Not far away they heard the rattle of oats in a pail and their father calling to his horse, "Sam, d'ye hear, you old devil? Come on up when I need you."

Eglantine and Nathaniel huddled together, hardly breathing. They heard the bridle rattling and Bud soothing the horse as he saddled him. "Steady, old boy. Steady now."

The saddling seemed to take an eternity. "Shh," Nathaniel shushed Eglantine when she merely raised her arm to push her glasses up on her nose. "Shh, he'll charge in here if anything moves," he warned.

It was a relief when they heard Bud saying,

"Well, which way d'ye think we should go, old man?" and they heard him take off through the bush.

"We'll go down the road," Eglantine whispered.

"Yeah, west," Nathaniel whispered back. "If she really was running away, Jasmin wouldn't stay on our land and she'd take Leroy where there'd be no people to laugh at him."

"Back into the mountains," Eglantine added as they dodged again, like crooks and adventurers, from shadow to shadow until they were out on the gravel road. "Be ready to dive down into the ditch if you hear anybody coming."

They walked close together down the rough twisting road, walking westwards toward the mountains, listening to the wild sounds of the moonlit darkness, peering into the shadows, never raising their voices to each other, always whispering.

"It's creepy," they agreed, sometimes holding hands and always waiting close by the other when they had to stop to shake pebbles out of their sneakers, and rub them out from between their toes.

"Wish we had horses," Eglantine said as they went round unfamiliar turns in the road.

"Or bikes," Nathaniel said longingly. "I'd come exploring down here if I had a bike—if I had a bike."

Eglantine snorted. "Who'd ever ride a bike on this road? Who'd ever get up the hill again, if they didn't fall off going down? A horse's better. Dad'll be miles away."

He was. He had opened a wire gate onto the

open field where Jasmin had met the lurking coyotes, and excited by the wild freedom of the moonlit night, he urged old Sam into a gallop round the fenceline, calling out "Yipee. Yippee," as he swung one arm high. He still kept a sharp gaze for any sign of his children having passed that way.

"Ought to do this more often, Sam, eh? old boy. This is better than being asleep in a hot old house, ain't it?"

He came to the place where Jasmin had first squirmed under the fence. "Something flattened the grass down here. What d'ye know?"

Then he swerved and zigzagged Sam, looking for a trail, laughing with the pleasure of the chase. "On the trail, now, boy. Like old times. Remember Hepsibah?" Bud felt young again and laughed at a memory of Olive, pretty and thin then, on her little mare. "Always was one for fancy names. Hepsibah! Can you beat that? Pity the little mare died, eh Sam, old boy?"

Sam snorted and reared at the fence.

"Jasmin. You down there?" Bud shouted then muttered her full name under his breath, "Jasmin Marie Antoinette! Okay, Sam, let's you and me find a gate and push through that trail. Something bin down there," he said soberly as he peered along the trail where Jasmin had struggled.

Down and round a few more twists in the road, Eglantine and Nathaniel paused by a wire gate pulled across a narrow overgrown road. The road led to an old house.

"It's a broken down old shack," said Nathaniel and was all for going on.

"No, come on," Eglantine urged him excitedly. "I bet they're in there. Bet they think they can live there. Come on, let's get them out." She was under the wire and halfway to the old building as she was speaking. Nathaniel hurried to catch up, pushing aside wild roses and clumps of heavy grasses.

Eglantine reached the broken window first and stood on tiptoe looking in and calling, "Okay, Jasmin, come on out. I know you're in there."

Nathaniel climbed up and was kneeling on the window ledge. "Can't see much. It's dark. All broken up things," he reported.

Eglantine was just pulling herself over the ledge when suddenly, without warning, a brilliant light shone behind them. Everything was lit up and they saw inside the cabin: broken floorboards with weeds growing out of them, a big cupboard crashed on the floor, an upturned table and broken chairs. In a flash they saw it all and in the same instant a massive black cat rushed between them and a deep voice boomed right behind them, "And what do you think you are doing? Trespassing on private property."

Eglantine and Nathaniel turned to look into the powerful flashlight and the stern face of a Mountie.

"And what are two Stalke children doing here?" he asked.

"Nothing," Eglantine said quickly and flashed Nathaniel a look to remind him that Bud and Olive had dinned it in to all the children that they mustn't talk family business outside the house.

"We was only exploring." Nathaniel smiled and tried to charm the Mountie with his angel face.

"If your parents haven't taught you that you don't go exploring on other people's property, it's time they did. Come on, walk. I'll take you home."

Sullenly they let the Mountie light them to his waiting car, and sullenly they endured the ride home in the quiet vehicle.

"Perhaps he'll just let us out at the gate?" Nathaniel whispered hopefully to his sister whose eyes were hard behind her spectacles.

No such luck. The Mountie knocked on the door until Olive, with a coat on over her nightie opened it, yawning.

"Good morning, Mrs. Stalke, I just picked up two of your children, wandering the countryside, trespassing. Not a good habit to let them get into, Mrs. Stalke. Two grizzlies have been seen in the district, you know."

"Oh, thank goodness you found them! Are they all right? We was real worried." For a moment it looked as if Olive was about to hug and kiss the Mountie. He backed off in time and she went on, "Their Dad's still out looking for them. He's been gone ages. I musta just dropped off to sleep. Oh, they're not in any trouble are they?"

"No, not this time Mrs. Stalke. And they're not hurt. Here they are. You see they get to bed, catch a bit of sleep before schooltime." He beckoned for the children to get out of the car.

"But that's not them. That's not them," Olive burst out.

"But, but, Mrs. Stalke," the Mountie stuttered, "what do you mean—'That's not them!'?"

"What I mean is that them's not the two what're missing." She shook her head and pointed her finger threateningly at the same time.

"Are you telling me—? Do you mean you've got two more out somewhere—missing?"

"You'd better believe it," Olive told him and she gave Nathaniel and Eglantine a funny look, very stern and very cross.

Nathaniel said quickly, "Oh Mom, we only went out to find Jasmin and Leroy."

Eglantine looked at her feet and let her hair fall forward, not wanting her mother to notice that the arm had come off her glasses again.

"Look, I'd better step inside and get all this sorted out, okay?" the Mountie insisted.

"Don't look at the mess," Olive said, then told him what she thought was the truth of the story of Jasmin and Leroy.

"I do hope Bud's found them. It's a big worry, two kids out on their own all night." Olive sighed as she finished her tale.

"It's a nice warm night, Mrs. Stalke," the Mountie said comfortingly. I'm sure no harm will have come to them—the two of them being together. However, Mrs. Stalke, I would like you to phone the police station as soon as your husband gets in— as soon as you have any news. If they're not home by schooltime—and I'm sure they will be—we'd better get a search started. Try not to get too alarmed, Mrs. Stalke. Remember—the two of them are together."

As soon as the Mountie left, Olive let her anger loose on Eglantine and Nathaniel. "What do you mean, eh? Two Stalke kids trespassing. Brought home by the police. Everybody knowing our business now because you two had to go and get caught out there. Git, git off to bed before your father comes in and sees your silly faces."

16

JASMIN WAS TOO UNNERVED BY THE DEATH OF THE spruce grouse to go out and pick strawberries, even though she felt certain that nobody was looking for her. She sat on her balcony playing with the clay, thinking her thoughts and talking to herself. "I don't feel like eating yet," she told her rumbling stomach.

At first it wasn't easy to concentrate on making a bear. Her eyes wandered to watch field mice scuttling, long-tailed and swift, about their business as the shadows lengthened across the crisp pine needles. The calls of the birds grew melodious as the day ended. The coyote pup looked innocent and peaceful, back in its shallow hollow, nose neatly tucked under tail. At sunset, the forest seemed only beautiful, not a place for killing and dying.

"I love it here," Jasmin murmured blissfully as the loveliness soothed her. "I love being alone with the trees and the little river. I love being alone."

Her fingers settled to work on the bulk of the bear. She bent over it frowning, wondering if she could ever get the heavy feeling of bear into a small clay sculpture.

"Reach up, bear, just like you did last night. I'll give you a tree to reach up." She stuck a thick twig in a mound of clay, prodding at the mound until it felt rough like pine needles, but different from the fur feel of the hulk of the bear's body.

It was almost dark before her fingers were satisfied with the bear. As she slipped it into the plastic drying bag with the porcupine and the curved coyote, she suddenly knew she was very tired.

"Such a lot has happened." She yawned, as she undressed, awkwardly kneeling, then slipped into the soft luxury of her red nightgown. She folded her day clothes carefully onto the shelf in the south wall. "Was it only last night," she asked herself, "that I put the kids to bed and decided to run away? Only last night! Can one day change a person so completely?" she murmured as she bent to take one more look at the shapes of her animals in their bag.

Like a dreamer she walked barefoot with her red gown trailing over the pine-needley earth as she went toward the whispering and gurgling rivulet to get her supper potato and to say goodnight to the coyote.

"So warm and so cool," she chanted and held her skirt out for a moment like a dancer doing a few steps while the last sleepy birds called. She sang, "Jasmin, Jasmin, this is like a princess in a storybook forest." Then she stopped her silly self, saying sarcastically, "Some princess! Crazy Jasmin."

She climbed into the shadows of her home, snuggled into her patchwork quilt on the piney, crunchy mattress, propped herself up on her parka pillow, crunched slowly on a juicy potato.

"Fingers, what shall we make tomorrow?" she mumbled sleepily, and thought of her grandmother's fingers making her quilt and red nightgown. "Perhaps clever fingers run in the family."

Jasmin's sleepy mind slipped about wondering if Grandmother was looking down from her heaven, seeing where the quilt and the gown had got to. Maybe she was giving Jasmin the skill from her fingers. Her mind slipped into the attic to look at Leroy and all the little kids sleeping and to ask who would fix the lunch pails in the morning? Who would wipe off the table and wash the dishes?

Sleep, however, soon took her mind from worrying about how the Stalke family would be managing without her, and Jasmin smiled, snug, safe and warm, sleeping blissfully her first hours in her own hiding-home.

Then she grew restless, her arms reaching out from under her quilt. She was dreaming, dreaming she was in a procession carrying her science project

101

in a big box toward the community arena at Witchitt. The box was heavy and slippery because her arms wouldn't reach all the way around it. "Oh, please don't let me drop it," she was crying out in her dream. Then a baby started wailing inside the box. All the schoolkids in the procession were mocking the baby, lifting up their faces, all of them wailing and screaming.

Just as the procession reached the double doors of the arena, and when the box was getting heavier and slipping till it bumped on her knees, three smooth brown bears rose up on their hind legs and waved their claws to guide the students in. One bear gave the box a lift so it was easier to carry. Just as she thought her troubles were over, all the students changed into prickly, sharp-faced animals, rushing round in a frenzy to find their names which had been stuck up all around the walls.

The box was heavy again. The Witchitt arena became a confusion of small rooms, each leading into a maze of more small rooms, and every room had a counter with students' names above it, showing them where to display their science projects. Everybody except Jasmin found a name. Her name wasn't there. The box was slipping. Soon she would have to drop it. She drifted painfully from room to room with every spiky-faced animal wailing at her in mockery. The baby in the box was wailing too. Then, when she was bent double, holding onto the box that had almost reached the floor, she saw her name.

For Meg was written in red, old-fashioned hand-writing. With a surge of strength she rushed toward the place and hoisted the heavy box onto her display space on the counter top.

She let go the box. But the counter top was not there. The box fell, down, down, down. The smell was terrible. It fell far down into the depths of the hole in the outhouse. As it disappeared Honey Angelina held up her little pink hands and in a ghostly and horrible voice wailed, "Jasmiiiin, Jaaasmiiin."

Jasmin woke up crying out. She was bathed in sweat. Where was she? Honey Angelina's face disappearing down the smelly hole filled her eyes.

The wailing was not a dream. It was still going on all around her. In the middle of the wailing she thought she heard a cry, Jaaaaasmiiiin. And the smell had not disappeared with the dream. It seeped into her den through the leafy curtain.

She lay quite still, breathing deeply, trying to get her bearings. Moonlight fell brightly through the gaps in her curtain, making lacy patterns on the balcony, on the quilt, and on the south wall shelves with the pot of violets. The golden edge of her poetry book glinted. *For Meg*—Oh yes, she thought, that's where one bit of her nightmare had come from. And it was real wailing that had got mixed up in her dream, for wasn't she at the edge of the world where the coyotes lived? As she lay there thinking how all the parts of her dream had got into her nightmare, some of the horror was eased and her body cooled down. She sat up and shook her head to try to get rid of the horrible sight of Honey Angelina

103

going down the hole. She concentrated on the baby asleep in her own cot in the pioneer bedroom.

As she calmed down, the wailing, the howling and yipping began to seem quite like wild, sad music. Jasmin held her hands out into the bright pattern of moonlight and moved them from shadow to light, light to shadow, like a dance, her magic hands in the moonlight. "We're safe. It was only a nightmare," she said softly so she could hear the normal sound of her voice. "If you want *to live as she did please* you have to get used to wild things. Remember, you're safe and secure here. Nothing's going to hurt you, and nobody's going to find you—see."

So saying, she made herself crawl out of her warmth to the edge of her balcony to spy out into the forest night that had mixed itself in her dream. "Ooh," she breathed in wonder as she saw the little coyote sitting in its place, its nose pointing to the moon singing, singing to the moon. And from every side there were answering coyote calls, high piercing notes quavering high into the sky. Jasmin sat down, amazed, to breathe in the scents of the night. Among them she caught the sweaty scent of an old bear. So, that was smell that got into her dream. She wrapped her arms around herself for warmth and giggled. It was all so simple and so satisfying to be solving problems. "If there was anyone to tell a story to," she said to the wailing night, "I should tell that a wild old bear tried to attack my den and my friend, the little coyote, warned it off and protected me. The little coyote saved the life of the sleeping princess." There she stopped and in a different voice snorted, "Some princess! Just because you're happy in the moonlight! Jasmin Stalke finds the end of the rainbow at the edge of the world where the coyotes live! You'd better get back to sleep. There's a lot to do tomorrow."

But back in her warm quilt, Jasmin was haunted again by her nightmare; the horror of Honey Angelina's face and her little pink hands falling down the hole made her squirm on the shushing pine needles. It was quite a while before the lullaby of coyote calls returned her to sleep in the cosy hiding-hollow behind the moonlit curtain of fragrant hanging branches.

17

"PERHAPS I'M STILL DREAMING," SHE WHISPERED AS she woke up, stretching her legs and wriggling her toes inside the cosy warmth of her quilt. A foot slipped out into the morning chill and she pulled it back into bed quickly.

"That's not a dream; that's real." She shivered and curled herself up again, peeking out with only a bit of her face to look around.

Gray mist floated in cloudy wisps through the green needles onto the balcony. "That looks like a dream. By myself, how can I be sure I'm not dreaming?" she asked herself. "Violets—I picked them and

made the pot, but *For Meg* was in my nightmare."
She took a big breath of cool forest morning air.
"It's real," she said with certainty. "Thank goodness, Honey Angelina down the hole was only a
dream."

The thought of Honey Angelina made Jasmin's
mind go worrying again back home. Poor Honey
Angelina. Poor Leroy. Poor everybody in the Stalke
house.

"But it's no good worrying about them," she
told herself miserably. They would soon learn to do
without her. Eglantine could be the oldest, getting
all the jobs to do and being Leroy's friend, couldn't
she?

Tears pricked her eyes at the thought of Leroy.
She must learn to put him out of her mind. Determinedly, she looked across to where her clay figures
were drying and made herself concentrate on coyotes, bears, porcupines—and the skill in her fingers.

In the bag with the models there was the rough
hunk of clay waiting to be made into things. She
pulled her arms out from under the quilt, flexed
her fingers, rubbed them into the palms of her hands,
and felt a sense of pleasure. But she didn't get up
right away; she lay back to enjoy the luxury of being
able to *live as she did please*.

Faintly the sounds of the rivulet slipped in with
the mist. Jasmin smiled smugly to think how lucky
she'd been to find a home with washing and drinking right beside it—and a nearness to berries and
mushrooms.

"Strawberries, blueberries, saskatoons, rasp-

106

berries," she listed the possibilities. "If you had any sense, Jasmin Marie Antoinette Stalke, you'd get up and see about getting in a food supply," she lectured herself as the thought of berries reminded her stomach it was hungry.

"But not until the housework's done. No eating or adventures till the work's done," she insisted as she crawled out into the chilly air. She dressed quickly, wearing her green parka as she swept every stray pine needle back into place in her mattress and spread the bright quilt neatly. Then she was ready to begin the day.

Outside, the mist was white and thick as though a cloud was low, enveloping everything. Even the nearest trees were faint as ghosts in a dream. The world was silent.

"It's safe," she breathed, convinced that nobody would be looking for her in such a mist. Anyhow, she thought gruesomely, by now they'd only be looking for the remains of a body that had been mauled by a bear, eaten by a cougar, or torn apart by coyotes. She laughed, a smug little laugh of victory.

"Do I dare go exploring?" She started an argument with herself.

"If you have any sense you'll stay right close to home."

"Don't be silly," she mocked herself. "Who do you think would be looking for you anyhow? Who cares about you, silly dummy?"

She decided it was okay to explore. So she set off, a lone traveler in the thick mist, eating a juicy potato slowly to make it last a long time. She only had three left. She whispered a few words to the little coyote who was still there like a watchdog. Then she was off slipping and climbing down the mist-floating slope. Mist lay wet on her eyelashes, and her sneakers and jeans were soon soaking, but she warmed up with the exercise. So, this morning she was an adventurer, a mountaineer, an explorer. This morning she was *brave as Margaret Queen and tall as Amazon*. A feeling of marvelous excitement made her want to shout and sing as she moved further away from her hiding-hollow and rivulet. Down, down, down, she slipped and climbed from ghost tree to ghost tree in the white cloud of mist. Then suddenly she was rolling, falling, trying to grab at grasses and stumps as she fell, and a roaring filled her ears. Crash and thump, she landed hard among rocks and boulders, and stood up, bruised and breathless, to see that she had landed on the rocky shore of the river.

The roar of the river was wild. It drowned out every other sound in the world. With the white mist hanging just above it, the rushing waters crashed and swirled over and around the rocks in the river-bed. Jasmin held her breath. It really was like being an explorer, seeing something fabulous for the first time in history.

As soon as she was accustomed to the booming sound, Jasmin climbed precariously across big rocks that raised dry heads out of the swirling waters, until she reached one she could sit on, an island in the flow and roar of the swift waters. She sat and hugged her knees, feeling like a sailor on a raging sea. She was hypnotised by the rushing river as it swirled past her.

Once, for a moment, a shaft of sunlight cut through the mist on the other side of the river and there was a quick glimpse of a wide valley stretching to the gray mountains. Jasmin saw wrinkles of snow gleaming like gold on the sides of the rugged mountains. Then the mist closed in again making a private world for Jasmin on her rock island. It was all like a dream. While she watched, hugging her knees, an antlered moose stepped out of the mist farther up the river, slow, dignified, step by slow step. Its big flat antlers were bold and heavy looking. Jasmin smiled because she could feel the fingers of her mind measuring the shape and mass of the moose as though she were already forming him in clay. She studied the bulk of his body, the angle and lift of the stepping legs. Would her fingers be clever enough to mold the flat, strong but delicate curve of those antlers? She wondered.

With slow dignity the moose walked chest deep into a pool by the bend of the river. He stood there, nosing the morning, unaware of her studying him. Jasmin kept still as moss on her rock downriver from him.

As though it wasn't enough to be sitting in a roaring river watching a moose, exactly opposite Jasmin, another wilderness miracle moment began to happen. She hugged her knees tighter and hardly breathed for fear of disturbing the moment. A doe and a spotted fawn had stepped delicately down to the river. Another perfect thing.

As she watched, the mist lifted briefly up the river beyond the moose, and Jasmin gasped. There stood a house. A peeled log house, bright yellow in a splash of sunshine. A house! That was terrible. She had been sure she was far, far away from houses and people.

And in the very instant that she felt the shock of seeing the house, she saw the plunge of a tawny orange cat. A cougar pounced onto the neck of the gentle doe. The doe dropped and crumpled. Its long legs twisted like broken strings. The lithe cougar dragged the doe away, a limp, furry heap.

Jasmin felt sick. It had happened so quickly. Uncertainly the small spotted fawn turned to follow the trail of its mother.

"No. No. No," Jasmin shrieked. But then, swift as fear, her voice was silenced. A great shadow whirled and twisted through the mist above the fawn. A clattering noise could be heard above the roars and rushes of the river. The fawn stood hypnotised in a new terror.

Jasmin hugged her knees tighter and tucked her head down hard. That clacking roar was a helicopter. It had swooped in low. Now it was hovering. Every instinct told Jasmin to keep perfectly still. She must not move. She must not be caught.

From up above, she could look like a plant in her green parka if she kept absolutely still. With her head tucked in, who could tell she was a human being? She stayed quite rigid, scarcely breathing. She would not be identified. She would not be caught.

18

SHE WAS FURIOUS AT HERSELF. WHY HADN'T SHE HAD
the good sense to stay hidden or at least to stay near
her hiding-hollow where she was safe? Now her heart
was throbbing enough to break her chest open and
burst through her eyes. She squeezed herself up
tighter and tighter, head tucked down. There wasn't
just the helicopter to worry about. What if somebody was watching from a high window in that tall
house? What was a house doing there? She had run
away to be far from people and civilization, hadn't
she? Fail. Fail. Fail. Her heart seemed to be thumping out the word FAIL. Well, she was *not* going to
fail at running away, see! She had to get back to her
hiding-hollow. Once she got there, nobody would
ever find her.

It seemed like forever that the helicopter hung
just above her. Then it moved a little bit further
down the river but she kept still. The pilot could
be looking back. It was only when she thought the
helicopter was a good distance away that she dived
across the perilous rocks of the riverbed and threw
herself down in a clump of tall grass and bushes.
She lay very still while she took stock of her position.
Through the tall grasses she saw that the fawn had
disappeared, the pool was empty of the moose. The
mist had thinned. The sun was fanning through it

and again she got a glimpse of the peeled log house with the sun reflecting off its windows. Then the helicopter roared and swept down again. She pushed her body and her face into the wet morning earth. The helicopter hovered, then swept away. Cunning as a wild animal, Jasmin made a short dash up the hillside, then flattened herself again. Like a soldier dodging bullets on a TV program, she made her way, dashing then flattening herself. Sometimes she wriggled along on her belly from bush to covering bush. She would not be seen. She would not be caught. Wild rose thorns grabbed at her clothes and tore blood drops out of the backs of her hands and her ankles. She was filthy and sweating by the time she was beyond the din of the racing river.

The helicopter went on swooping and hovering like a trailing hawk so she knew for certain she was being hunted.

She was angry with herself. She should have seen that the mist was lifting. Stupid thing, Jasmin! Doubly stupid because she couldn't be exactly certain where she had made her way down the slope. It all looked different from below and she began to panic. Where was her gully? Her rivulet? Suppose she couldn't find her home?

Next time the helicopter sped off farther down the river she made a longer dash, then dragged herself up and to the left where she thought the gully must be. Her hands were bleeding and she was covered with mud.

She had to wait out another swoop of the helicopter, head down in the wet earth, heart thumping.

Her next dash brought her to the side of her gully, to the gentle sound of her own rivulet. She flopped down with her face on a cool rock, rested a moment and listened to the helicopter clacking steadily farther down the river, making echoes across the sky. Disturbed squirrels were chittering everywhere, raising an angry commotion in the treetops.

Cautiously and slowly, Jasmin raised her head to locate her hiding-hollow. Her eyes searched the hillside but they found nothing she recognised. Where was she? She looked around helplessly as she heard the helicopter approaching for another low sweep.

Then, before it was above her, there was a sharp yelp from below, farther down the gullyside, and she saw the little coyote. My friend, she thought. My friend guiding me home. And she believed it. She had been looking up the gully when, all the time, her den was in the other direction. She could see, now, the bend of the jackpine that was the roof over her balcony.

When the helicopter went away again, she checked carefully that nothing of hers was visible through her pine branch curtain. She checked to be sure her larder was undisturbed. Then she climbed home to safety.

"Thank you, little coyote," she whispered, "thank you for guiding me home." She wanted to believe that the coyote was truly her friend but her sensible mind kept laughing at her and telling her that wild animals don't show people the way home. "You're crazy, Jasmin Stalke," she said to herself.

"But never mind, you're home, safe and sound. Now, don't take any more risks." Out of sheer relief, she was babbling to herself. Just as she was about to flop down on her patchwork quilt she saw the filthy mess she was in. She was muddy and stinking.

Jasmin wrinkled up her nose as she looked at her filthy hands and mud-covered parka and jeans. How horrible! She must have dragged herself through all sorts of dirt and animal droppings. She was sure she smelled like ten old bears and five coyotes. She would have to get down to the rivulet and clean herself up. But, no. The helicopter was still circling around. The squirrels were in a noisy state of disturbance. The coyote was nowhere to be seen. Everywhere the birds were a-twitter. "Take no risks, Jasmin Marie Antoinette Stalke," she warned herself. But, oh, what was she to do?

She must get way back in her hiding-hollow and lie low until all the signs of danger had passed. So she cleaned her hands, grimacing in disgust, on the backs of her jeans then got out of her filthy clothes. She wiped the mud off herself as best she could on her T-shirt, and put on her red gown. That felt better.

She rolled her muddy clothes into a bundle where they wouldn't show from outside and then scrunched down on her bed, waiting for her body to calm down. The helicopter was still clattering round the sky and every animal was crying warning.

"What a fuss for nothing," Jasmin muttered to herself. "Why don't they just leave me alone?" She thought of her mother and father being upset and stuck her chin out hard. "They've got enough other children to take my place. Anyhow, it'll do Eglantine good to do her share of the work. Poor Leroy!" She wondered if Eglantine would be nice to him and wipe off his mouth.

And suddenly her mind was back in the *for everything room*. She could see everything, touch everything, open the fridge door with a click and get a mug full of cold milk from the heavy yellow jug. She could walk over and change channels on TV. She could see her mother dropping tears on Honey Angelina's head. Could her mother feel her presence there? "If you think hard enough, can you put yourself in another place?" she wondered. She imagined herself at her desk in the classroom. She moved her fingers over the old scratchings and drawings on the desk top. Funny! Did the teacher know that Jasmin Stalke was sitting at her desk? Maybe if you imagined hard enough you could make it real, she reasoned.

She began to wonder how long she would have to stay scrunched up and hiding as the disturbance continued in the trees and sky all around her.

To pass the time, she studied the roots that were like veins in the ceiling of her hollow. She watched a spider spinning a web from the pine-bough curtain across to the shelves where her violets showed dark blue against the brown of the rock and the brown leather of the *For Meg* book.

Time seemed to slow down. She held up her hands and rubbed at the smudges where the rose thorns had pricked blood. She studied her hands, her fingers, still surprised by the imagination she had discovered in them. They could feel the top of her scarred desk, they could feel the bulky body of the moose stepping to the edge of the river—and the dandelion-clock silky softness of Carmen Miranda Elisa's hair, and the hard strength of Leroy's hands.

"Stop it. Stop it," she told herself as her eyes smarted with tears. "Think about something else."

The helicopter made another roaring swoop. She lay back on her bed and looked to where her clay models were drying. "Think about the marvelous hands of Jasmin Marie Antoinette Stalke," she ordered, adding, "At least I think they're marvelous. Marvelous for me." She gazed at her little figures with satisfaction, rolled on the bed and laughed quietly. "Nobody will ever find me, ever, ever, ever. I love it here."

She pulled her clay over to her and began to knead a lump of it. What should she make next?

The moose and deer with their long thin legs, and especially the complicated antlers of the moose, wouldn't come to her fingers. Instead, they worked off their nervousness and got into practice with the simple shape of the coyote as it had sat nose lifted to the moon, howling up into the night.

As she worked, the helicopter sounds grew faint and far away but the squirrels continued to chatter out warnings and a hawk cackled and cried. She had learned her lesson and had no intention of venturing out again until all was calm and the coyote had returned to lie curled up and trusting.

116

She kneeled, peeked out through the curtain, and saw there was no sign of her watchdog. Her stomach was rumbling with hunger. "You'll have to wait," she told it.

But it was a long time. The sun moved round in the sky to bathe her side of the valley in golden afternoon warmth. There was nothing else to do but keep her fingers working. She spread all her creatures out along the edge of her bed, lay down with her eyes on their level, and was surprised again by her skill. Two coyotes, a porcupine and a reaching bear. And while her fingers had been shaping and putting the detail on the second coyote, her mind had thought of a way to solve the problem of the doe's long legs.

She felt dance-y and sing-y inside as she began working on a complicated mix-up of cougar and dead doe. She collapsed the doe with its stiff legs onto the side of the sturdy cougar. That way there were no brittle ends of clay to break off. She watched the small sleek head of the cougar grow out of her fingers, and its lithe haunches and hard muscles. Pity and misery absorbed her as her fingers struggled round the helpless, undignified form of the dead doe. Very fiddly. Jasmin kept changing position as her legs got stiff from sitting on them and her bottom got pins and needles. She had to keep setting the model down, lying back to study it from eye level, turning it round so she could consider all sides of it. She forgot her hunger, forgot everything except the demands of the problem of getting her feelings into the powerful killer and the crumpled doe. She had forgotten that she was a hunted creature herself until—

A hawk cackled, strident and near. There was a crashing sound. A riot of disturbances.

With her model in her hands, Jasmin pulled back hard against the wall of the sleeping-alcove, trying to be so still that the pine needle mattress would not crunch. She held her breath.

Outside there were men's voices.

19

A DOG YAPPED AND YELPED—VERY NEAR. IT SOUNDED like a little dog. But it was under her balcony.

Jasmin pressed herself against the uneven hardness of the rocky wall and held her breath, panic making her weak. She hadn't thought of being tracked down by dogs.

But wait—the dog wasn't pawing up onto her balcony. It seemed to be backing off, moving away, yapping continuously. She dared to breathe.

"Please, please, nobody must find me," she pleaded silently while her heart drummed in her ears.

Rocks slid down the hillside. Branches snapped. Pine needles crunched as heavy feet jumped and slid on them. Men's voices sounded, right beside her.

"Stinks of bear," one said roughly. Not a voice she knew.

Another voice answered, "That's it. That's what's setting that dog a'mine off. Don't like no truck with them bears, she don't. Won't hang around where there's bin a bear."

The first voice again. "An' meself, I don't reckon no kids 'ud hang around down here. Spooky. Godforsaken place. Reckon we're wasting our time down here."

"No. Guess you're right. Don't see no sign of any kid down here."

"An' I reckon the copter's done a pretty thorough search. Bin all over here, I should think."

"Wasting our time. Pretty sharp lookout them copters keep. Not much gets away from them. Reckon we should get back up?"

"Sure. No kid I've ever known 'ud be down here. Scare 'em to death. Any kid 'ud turn back home soon as it got dark."

"Unless a cougar dropped 'em down. Plague of cougars, they say, this year."

"But never heard tell of 'em attacking folks."

"Kids is pretty little folks, mind you. Wouldn't surprise me if—"

"Well, if a cougar has—well, ain't much use in looking anyhow."

The feet, the voices, the yapping dog were moving away. The cougar and doe shook on Jasmin's trembling hand, as she stayed with her back to the rock not knowing whether to laugh or cry. "It's a nice place here. It's a nice place here," she whispered to herself almost hysterically. "They didn't find me. They didn't find me. I'm safe, safe, safe."

She sniffed the air. Bear smell? It must have been on her filthy rolled-up clothes. Everything was working out luckily for her now.

Her stomach rumbled loudly. "Oh!" She moved uneasily, thinking how terrible it would have been if her stomach had made those noises when the men were near.

Her body was crying out for food, but there was no peace outside yet. *"No breakfast had she many a morn, No dinner many a noon, And 'stead of supper she would stare Full hard against the moon,"* Jasmin said, to bolster her courage. "But I hope I don't have to wait that long, not until the moon is out."

To take her mind off hunger she returned to work some more on the clay, wondering if she could ever complete the cougar and doe to her satisfaction. If she concentrated, perhaps the hungry feeling of her own body would get through her fingers and into the skin of the cougar.

"Now I'm hungry, perhaps I understand the feeling to kill," she breathed. "Perhaps I shall kill and eat dragonflies—and frogs—and caterpillers— and flies—and beetles. Ugh!"

Such thoughts gradually left her as she settled down to the job of perfecting the complicated model of wild strength and death, and, while she was totally absorbed, time passed. When at last she set the sculpture down, feeling that it was finished, she was so lost in her daze of creation that fear of capture, even the sense of hunger, was forgotten.

"Oh, I like it. I love it," she cried out faintly, as again that dance-y, sing-y feeling spread through her. "Have *I*, really I, made that?" She lay back on her quilt, swaying her hands in the air. "Clever, clever things," she whispered to them, and at the same time kicked her toes out of her red gown. She smiled with pleasure at her collection of animals. "Oh, but I'm hungry," she said as her stomach gurgled again. She lay still and listened.

Silence. No helicopter. No squirrels, or hawks, or other birds. No sound except the hot afternoon whisper and tinkle of the rivulet. No other sound at all. It was as though all of nature was holding its breath. Not a movement of leaf, of breeze or of birds' wings. The silence was almost oppressive. Jasmin knelt cautiously on her balcony and looked out. Maybe it would be all right to venture out now. The coyote was back but not curled and easy. The coyote was stretched out long. It was panting, its thin sides going in and out. Surely it was safe to part the branches. Jasmin stuck her head out and looked all around. Nothing moving. Absolute silence and stillness everywhere. So the search must be over. It was safe to go out, eat, wash, clean her stinking clothes. The hot sun would soon dry everything. Why did it feel strangely ominous?

Even though there was no sign of danger, this time Jasmin kept totally alert, soundless except for her soft whispering to the coyote. Looking and listening carefully all the time, she took her clothes and her muddy sneakers down into the gully with her when she went to her larder. Even her movements caused no disturbance around her so she sat by the rivulet with her feet in the icy current to eat her potato slowly, dipping it into the clear water to make it colder and juicier. She cupped her hands and drank a lot of the water to fill up the hungry space inside her because, even though she made it last a long time, the potato only whetted her appetite and made her determined to search around to replenish her larder once she had done her washing and got it out to dry. She mustn't eat another potato until she had other things to put in her larder. There were only two potatoes left and she knew she had to be prepared to make them last a long time, or even keep them for any emergency.

She decided that rather than go further away from her hiding-hollow to find deeper water for her washing, she would do it just a few steps downstream. As she spread her jeans, T-shirt, underwear and sneakers on the rocky bottom of the rivulet for the waters to cascade over, a hot heavy silence hung oppressively in the air all around her. It was awkward trying to keep her long gown out of the water and she didn't want to get it, her last piece of clothing, wet. She held it up with one hand and tried rubbing the grime off the front of her parka with the other hand. She poured handfuls of water on the worst places and rubbed with her free hand but her efforts only spread the mess. She hoped the flow of water over the other things was loosening the dirt but she didn't quite know how to deal with the bulky green parka.

Thinking about it, she climbed to the top of the gully again and looked around. It seemed safe. The coyote was still there stretched out, panting. The silence hung heavy. She went back again and decided she might as well spread the parka in the water as she had done the other things. She felt certain it wasn't the right thing to do with a parka. But the sun would soon dry it. It was hot as an oven. For some reason the silence began to fill her with a growing sense of uneasiness.

As she watched the water collecting on the green cloth of her nylon parka, first making pools on it then spreading through it, she remembered a film she had once seen in school where women tread their washing in a river to get the dirt out. That seemed like a good idea. The heat and the silence made her think it was quite safe to take her gown off to keep it dry and leave her hands free. She hung it on a root nearby on the gullyside. Then she paddled up and down on her mushy parka, curling her toes over the gucky places. The clear water was stained brown before it was carried away in the gurgling currents round smooth rocks.

What a luxury to be naked in the hot sun. She had an idea. She could have her first ever private bath, with no one to watch and no little kids to put matchsticks and plastic things to float in the water. She checked the top of the gully again, checked that the silence was still perfect. It was. Nothing stirred.

Not a leaf trembled. It was as though a hot, still sleep had wrapped around the world. So, feeling secure, she lay face down in the water, opened her eyes in it and was delighted by the tricks and distortions the water and sunlight played with the colors and shapes of rocks and pebbles. Then she turned over and tipped her head back so her hair was washed by the stream. What a marvelous life, she thought, now she *lived as she did please*. She stood up and shook her hair, then in happiness, lifted her arms to the sun and twirled round and round in the water swinging her heavy wet hair.

She had better get her washing trodden clean, she decided, and hung out to dry before it was too late. Tomorrow it could easily rain and then she'd be left with only her gown to wear if the other things weren't thoroughly dried.

So, like the women she had seen in the film at school, she trod the dirt out of her clothes while the sun was drying her thick long hair. She began to think that the parka was never going to give up all its dirt and stains. Her sneakers, though, were beginning to look clean under the water. Then suddenly, "What's that?" she asked, catching her breath. Strange sounds. Something far away like a swish of fizzing, rolling waters. Before she had time to work out what was happening, the swishing became a roar. The treetops bent, twisted and tossed. She was forced up against the gully side, where she caught hold of a thick root or she would have been flung into the air.

A massive wind was surging through the hot silence. She could not stand against it. The tree-tops tossed in a lashing frenzy of madness. The whole hillside seemed to be bending, breaking, roaring.

Oh, her nightgown! Her beautiful red gown. It was picked up and tossed like torn paper, before it was blown away up the hillside. Seeing that, Jasmin went wild as a tiger, fighting the wind, breathless and panting, leaping and battling to catch up with her treasured gown. It caught for a moment on a branch. But before she could reach it the wind began to pelt her bare body with hailstones as hard as bullets. She managed to grab the gown and wrench it free, pulling it quickly over her head and down onto her body to protect her. Then she struggled against the biting hail, trying to protect her arms, her face and head, until she reached the calm and safety of her hiding-hollow.

By the time she had got her breath, the afternoon was caught up in a thrashing, screaming storm. Thunder cracked above and lightning made wild flashes. Hailstones big as baseballs were slung at the hillside, lashing at her pine-bough curtains. A few stones bounced and crashed onto her balcony and into her hollow. But it was all right. She was safe. She was a watcher in a cosy place. So the storm became fun.

It was wild, better than television because it was real, like a storm at sea, like an earthquake. It was a natural disaster and she was part of it. Trees and branches were breaking and snapping. In just a few minutes the hillside had turned white, covered by a raging, running, bouncing torrent of hailstones, deep as a heavy snowfall.

Jasmin laughed to think of the good pounding her garments were getting in the water. Every last bit of filth should be getting knocked out of them.

She lay on her stomach looking out into the storm. It tossed the curtain boughs, hissed and raged.

"If only I'd picked up another potato, or some mushrooms," she groaned longingly, before she caught on to the idea of sucking hailstones.

"Hmm. Like popsicles, like ice cream, like treats," she said sucking and munching happily. "I love this place. I love living here. I love wild storms. I love being alone . *Alone with her great family, She lived as she did please.*"

20

"BUT, BUD, YOU SAID THEY'D COME BACK AS SOON AS they was cold and hungry," Olive cried, while tears ran down her white face onto Honey Angelina's fluffy head.

Bud was mad as well as worried. His ride through the night and the forest hadn't made him into a cowboy hero. He'd had to come back without finding a sign of his two children. He'd turned back because when the forest got so thick and black he couldn't believe that any kids would keep going through it. He was sure he was on the wrong trail. As though that wasn't bad enough he got home to find the Royal Canadian Mounted Police knew the kids had hoofed it.

He had to admit to himself he was worried but he wasn't going to admit it to anybody else yet. He sounded his usual irritable self when he answered Olive. "Why don't you do something useful, woman, like get the coffee on. Save your tears for when they're needed." Then he turned on his children, crossly yelling, "You kids had better get some dry clothes on before you all catch your death of cold. Don't you think there's enough for your mother to worry about?" They had all been out in the storm and were dripping wet.

In all the goings-on nobody took any notice of Bud. Eglantine thought it was all pretty exciting. At school, before the storm, the Stalke kids had been made to feel important, everybody asking them questions, and one of the teachers had mended Eglantine's glasses with crazy glue so nobody could tell they'd been broken.

Now the Stalke house itself was getting important with men who were coming in out of the rain with their guns. One man had a little dog that had sneaked inside and kept shaking itself all over Carmen Miranda Elisa and Marigold Lolita May. They loved it, and were squealing with laughter.

Men stood at the door shaking their dripping jackets and taking off their mud-caked boots before they stepped inside.

"Never seen hailstones that size afore in my life," one man said as he came in.

"Just once I remembers, back in 1927," an old cowboy added.

Nathaniel couldn't resist joining in. "Coulda killed you if you got one on the head. Hope Leroy put a bucket on his head." Nathaniel thought he was making a joke but his mother moaned at him, "Don't you dare say that. Don't you dare talk about people getting killed."

"Yep. You just watch what you're saying, will you," Bud warned and had another go at taking Olive's mind off her troubles. "Olive," he said, "these men need some coffee. Get with it, eh?"

The hail had turned to rain and everybody stood around in the Stalke *for everything room* watching the heavy downpour bouncing off the wrecked cars and the junky machinery. The ground was a mush of mud and hail and rain. Everybody was wet and the grownups were worried and uncomfortable, trying to think of something to say. Some of the men had already given up hope of ever seeing Jasmin and Leroy alive again, only they weren't going to say so.

They all turned to watch TV when the news came on with the latest report on the missing rural children. Jasmin's last school photograph was flashed onto the screen.

"Nice looking kid," the old cowboy said and

that made Olive's tears gush out again. Everybody stared at Jasmin's picture except Eglantine. She went over to the little mirror to comb her hair and take a look without her glasses on. She must be a good-looking kid too, if Jasmin was.

There wasn't a picture of Leroy. The newsman described him as a husky eleven-year-old, big for his age, albino and retarded.

Olive cried out to everybody, "Bud, he said they'd be sure to come home when they was cold and hungry." None of the men knew what to say because they were wondering what harm had come to the kids, if they had been murdered, or killed by wild animals. But the old cowboy did his best to make everybody feel better. He nodded to everybody and said, "Guess they'll be coming home soon, lady, 'cause they'll be good and wet. Ain't a dry thing for miles."

"An' it don't look like letting up none," Bud said as he stood in the open doorway watching the thudding rain and the heavy sky.

"But you said they'd come home when they was good and hungry," Olive sobbed. "They must be good and hungry by now." She still hadn't made the coffee and the floor was wet and swimmy.

21

THE RAIN SHOWED NO SIGN OF EASING. IT BEAT DOWN, slashing and hissing, washing away every last white trace of hailstones, churning the hillside into a moving mass of mud and rushing, cascading surface streams.

Jasmin waited and waited for it to stop until the time came when she had to go out. Surely nobody would be searching for her in the downpour. She poked her head out through the branches of her dripping curtain to look and listen, to make certain it was absolutely safe to venture out. Wetness trickled down her neck and ran down her nose, but there was no sound except the wild rushing of many waters.

The coyote was not there.

"It wouldn't stay there in the wet, would it now?" Jasmin ridiculed herself, "getting its coat soaked. And I'd better not get my only dry garment wet, had I?" She slipped out of her red gown. She was pretty certain she was safe.

She shivered, then laughed joyously as the rain pelted down all over her. "Crazy, crazy!" The mud was nicely squishy under her toes. She played around for a second or two giggling, dancing a bit and saying over to herself crazily, *"She lived as she did please,* she did, *She lived as she did please!"* Then she saw that her gully had gone wild; the tiny rivulet had swollen into a raging torrent reaching up its banks. What about her clothes? She knew exactly where she had left them, exactly where she had been paddling on her parka. She *had* to find them. In desperation she plunged into the water, then gasped and reeled. The cold stopped her breath and made her cry out. The current would have knocked her off her feet if she hadn't clung to an overhanging branch. The water tore at her legs and swirled round her hips.

She knew it was crazy to try—crazy and dangerous—but she had to find her clothes. Reaching out from the branch she summoned all her strength to hold herself steady. With the current pulling at her, she tried to feel around the rocks with her feet. Pebbles crashed hard against her ankles. As her feet searched she tried to peer down through the water for signs of her clothes but the water was brown and angry. She didn't stand a chance against the savage push and pull of the torrent.

Get out while you're still alive, her sensible voice was telling her. But at the same time a horrified idea was filling her mind. She could just see the news on TV with the news man shouting, "The naked body of a girl was found." How terrible if they showed a picture. She'd hate that. All the boys at school seeing. And her desperate voice was screaming in her head, *You've got to find your sneakers; you've got to find your clothes. You can't live without clothes.*

With amazing strength she pushed herself

deeper into the stinging cold of the tugging water, struggling to keep upright while her feet searched for a garment or a shoe. She knew that the current must have washed everything away, yet she didn't want to believe such a terrible thing.

But it was true. Her clothes were gone. Her larder had broken away. Everything she depended on had vanished. She pulled herself back up on the bank and rested for a moment, shivering.

She was blue with cold and breathing hard when she got back to the safety of her den. She rolled herself up for warmth and protection in the soft rough friendliness of her patchwork quilt and scrunched herself against the back wall of her hollow.

She could scarcely think straight. Nothing was left but a nightgown and a patchwork quilt. Then, as though it was from far away, she heard her voice saying, as it had said to the bear, over and over, *a chip hat had she on, a chip hat had she on*. She reached out and put her hat on her wet hair and pulled it down hard on her head. She still had her broken hat, her clay and her marvelous models, the thin book and a few violets in a jar.

Suddenly she was exhausted. It was too much for her mind to cope with. She sank down into the coziness of her quilt and pine needles still wearing the hat and muttering over and over to herself desperately, *a chip hat had she on,* as sleep pulled her away from her problems.

22

OLIVE WAS NEARLY OUT OF HER MIND WHAT WITH one thing and another. Everybody was tracking mud in all the time. There was no school because the bridges were out, leaving the roads useless. When the kids were not out searching and getting soaked to the skin, they were underfoot. Wet clothes were draped from chairbacks, all over the chesterfield, on hooks and door handles.

Nathaniel, who was switching the TV from station to station to see all the news bulletins, was shouting his own commentary to anybody who was listening. "It says we've had the worst summer storm in fifty years."

Eglantine tossed her wet hair and shouted across the muddle and din, "So what's new? Tell us something we don't know."

Nothing daunted, Nathaniel tried again. "It says the rain ain't going to stop. Why don't we build an ark?"

"Why don't you be quiet," Bud snapped.

Nathaniel left the picture on, news shots of Dandron's Main Street, with cars up to their axles in water. A newscaster shouted that thousands of dollars worth of damage had been done to basements. "Fortunately there has been no loss of life reported," he bellowed cheerfully.

Olive cried.

Eglantine took that moment to chirp in. "Do I get to sleep in Jasmin's bed yet?"

Olive screamed at her. "If you ever ask that question again, Eglantine girl, I won't answer for what these hands'll do to you. Your sister's coming back to sleep in her own bed, don't you ever forget it."

Bud gave Olive a strange, sad look. "I hopes you're right," he muttered then carried on almost to himself, "I don't know where else to look. When I ran away, it sure never lasted like this."

Another television station announced that the telephones in the Dandron district were out of service. "Rural communities are completely cut off. The Royal Canadian Mounted Police warns against travel on any rural road. The thick mud is treacherous."

Olive whimpered and Honey Angelina began bawling.

Nathaniel switched to another channel where another newscaster announced, "Weather conditions are hampering the search for two children missing for five days. No let-up in the rain is forecast in the near future. More on this after these commercials." A choir burst into song about furniture.

'I don't care what they say," Olive cried hysterically. "I know my two kids are coming back."

"Hush up, you'll only upset yourself." Bud tried in his awkward way to comfort her. "Maybe you're right, Oli."

"I know I'm right." She shuddered. "I can feel

it in my bones, my two kids'll be back in their own beds. My Jasmin's got a lot of sense and she's a good girl with Leroy. She'll look after Leroy. The two of them together, they'll be all right. They'll come home again, I tell you all. I can feel it in my bones."

But no matter how hard or loud Olive insisted, her eyes stayed red and swollen with crying.

23

THE STEADY RAIN FELL AND FELL. THE RIVULET raged and spread its waters wider on the hillside where broken branches, mounds of mud, and gobs of pine needles turned the wilderness into a disaster.

Jasmin had lost count of time. Days and nights both seemed like dreaming time. She slept a lot. The first terrible pangs of hunger had gone away to be replaced by a weakness and a dreamy floating feeling. She found it hard to finish her own thoughts. "When the rain stops—I must—"

"When the rain stops I—must—"

When the rain stopped she would have to solve her problems of food and clothing—"when the rain stops." She knew she was good at solving problems for she had watched her fingers solve clay problems like the lanky legs of the doe and the fawn. They had made a giant moose with antlers. Antlers had been a big problem. After the antlers her fingers had managed the delicate fanned tail of the male spruce grouse. "When the rain stops I shall be—able to solve all my problems—when the rain stops."

Every so often she gathered her strength and took little naked walks into the pounding rain. Well, not quite naked; she wore her chip hat. Even in her weak and dreamy state she knew she must keep her red gown, her only clothing, dry. She chewed on leaves and grasses and on the delicacy of faintly perfumed, rain-bedraggled rose petals. The rain had brought out strange mushrooms. She ate any she could find that weren't too bitter, even some that she had never seen before. She knew they couldn't be poisonous because her mother had made all the children learn which ones could kill them. There weren't many of those in Alberta, her mother said. Even though she felt so strange and dreamy, even though she felt as though she was flying instead of walking, she did remember a lot of sensible things. She kept reciting the provinces of Canada from east to west, then from west to east to make sure her mind was still working. Also, she remembered not to go far away from her home without her clothes on. She knew that she would feel awful if searchers found her without clothes. But she also knew that it was harder and harder to be quite sure what was real and what was dreaming. There were times when the clay animals grew larger than life size and moved toward her. Now, that had to be a dream.

She thought it was real that sometimes a wet, scraggly coyote followed her in the rain while she whispered to it. Was it only a dream that sometimes it stood on its hind legs and pushed its sharp quivering nose in through her branches? Was it a dream that once, in the pouring rain, she crawled in the mud on her knees with her hair running rivers, moving slowly toward the coyote, whispering, until her nose touched the coyote nose? The pointed teeth were terrifying but the eyes were timid and the nose cold and quivering. Was it real that the coyote quick-licked her mouth, then ran away? "A dream, Jasmin, just a dream," her floating mind told her. "It couldn't be real because wild animals are proud and private, like a strong moose in the river in the morning."

She lay back on her bed and drifted into a dream. Mr. Podluck the school principal was flying after her like a hawk only he was wearing a long striped shirt and yellow cowboy boots. He was cackling and squawking the terrible word *fail, fail, failfailfailFAIL.* He was chasing her up against the ceiling of the school auditorium and she had to keep holding her red gown down to stop it from blowing up and showing her bare bottom. He was trying to make her take a black report card. He kept pushing it at her, cackling, *Fail. Fail. Fail.* She was screaming because she couldn't get away from him. He had nearly caught her and put the report card in her hand when suddenly there was a window in the dark ceiling and she flew through it with a great crashing. The broken glass splintered into dazzling flying stars as she soared away into the brilliant dark sky. She flew into her own waking, believing she could still hear the glass crashing, but it was only the rain. And

137

gray sky was breaking into her hiding hollow. The branches were parting and a head was pushing in. She screamed and hoped she was dreaming.

Jasmin sat up and clutched her quilt to her chin. She pressed her back against the hard wall to give herself strength, struggling to figure out if this was a dream or a real thing.

The head that pushed in was covered with black hair, dripping water down a face with a beard and dripping water off big black eyebrows. Silver water dripping onto her balcony. Was she dreaming? Another face floated in like a rose petal dripping with silver water. Was it real?

Jasmin felt her eyes filling with the silver water and the faces on her balcony blurred and quivered but they didn't go away. It wasn't a dream. It was real. What could she do?

She stuck out her tough chin and stared fiercely into the faces through the silver water that was filling her eyes. She opened her mouth and shouted as loud as she could but her voice seemed to be coming from far away. "Go away. Leave me alone," she shouted faintly. "Go away."

She knew who they were, those faces. Everybody round Dandron knew who they were. They were THEM PEOPLE.

24

EVERYBODY KNEW THAT THEM PEOPLE WERE TER-rible strangers. Jasmin knew because everybody said so.

"Why are THEM PEOPLE sticking their heads in on my balcony if it isn't a dream? Why would they be poking their noses into my business if it isn't a dream?" Jasmin's faltering thoughts asked.

Her mind seemed to have broken into pieces and shattered like the window in the auditorium ceiling in the Mr. Podluck dream. Everything was all mixed up and floating strangely. It was like TV with the sound turned off. Like football in slow motion. Only it was in her mind that the sound had been turned off. So, she thought, "I am in a dream with silent slow motion." The mouths of THEM PEOPLE opened and closed, making no sound.

Jasmin's dazed mind jumped to Main Street in Dandron where all the kids were mocking THEM PEOPLE, jumping up at the windows of their van to try to see what was inside. THAT WOMAN was swishing around in a long skirt with her red hair braided long down her back. THAT MAN's black beard was sparkling now like a forest with raindrops. Rivulets poured off the thick eyebrows like waterfalls off mountains. Black hairs grew like wet spiders on the back of his floating giant hand.

Jasmin felt herself floating toward the rose-petal face with wet freckles and swimmy green eyes. In a dream she was sipping sweet hot milk and a hand was stopping her from gulping. The milk floated warm in her chest and the giant hairy hand held her clay porcupine in the valley of its palm. She wanted to scream and stop him from hurting the porcupine. Everybody knows hairy giants do terrible things.

The giant's black brows frowned and his fierce black eyes asked a terrible silent question. She couldn't do anything, but watch as the giant hands caught all her floating animals and wound them in wide bandages that seemed to float out of a green backpack. The giant hands buried the bandaged animals in the green bag with her gold-edged book.

Then the dream changed and she was floating through the sky and the rain with her bright quilt flying like a canopy. She was sucking a sugar candy that was divine. She was flying away with THEM PEOPLE. Even in her dream she knew it was wrong to fly away with THEM PEOPLE because everybody knew they did terrible things.

They *did* terrible things.

They let her fall in deep cold water that pulled and pulled at her to get her into their black cave.

The water tugged at her gown, tore at her legs and tried to get away with her chip hat. She fought to stop them from taking away her chip hat.

She screamed and fought but THEM PEOPLE held her down. They pushed her down into the blackness of their terrible cave.

Blackness.

Everything was blackness.

25

HANA AND JULES WERE THE PEOPLE KNOWN AROUND Dandron, suspiciously, as THEM PEOPLE. They lived in the tall house of peeled logs that Jasmin had seen on the other side of the river, shy and private persons who chose to live in the wilderness. They were newcomers to a district where the other inhabitants had all been born and raised, and they were different. They both wore their hair long and Jules was the only man around with a beard. Nobody really knew much about them although everybody had opinions and gossip and stared at the two strangers when they drove into Dandron once a week to buy provisions.

Just before the storm, before the roads and bridges were washed out, and before the earth had been turned to mud, the Royal Canadian Mounted Police had called on them to question them about two missing children.

"Well, they sounded as though they were accusing us of kidnapping them," Hana exclaimed indignantly when at last the uniformed men had gone away.

"Sure did," Jules agreed. "I can't help feeling sorry for the kids—being hunted."

"You know"—Hana sighed thoughtfully—"there must be some very good reason for their running away or they'd have crept back the very first dark, scary night."

"Oh, I don't know, Hana. Maybe they're not in the wilderness. Maybe they hitchhiked into the city, or holed up with friends. Anyhow, would you have run back home when you were a kid because of the dark?"

"Oh, no, no no!" Hana laughed. "Of course I wouldn't. I'd have loved it. And, of course, I'd have been too proud to let myself get caught—"

"That's what I thought," Jules nodded. "I wonder what we should do if they are out this way—although I haven't seen or heard a sign of them."

"About all we can do is put out some food and a sign to them—just in case they are hereabouts and in trouble," suggested Hana

That's what they had done, put out a tin box on the balcony containing nuts, dates, some apples and a loaf of fruity bread. They'd also made a fairly big sign and left it by the food: *FOOD HERE. WE WILL HELP YOU IF YOU NEED US.* In smaller letters the message was printed, *Your parents say, "Please come back. We love you."*

Jules and Hana had debated about putting the last message on because they had no idea what sort of parents the missing children had. "And parents are often the last persons to know what is really troubling a child," Hana mused.

However, after all their trouble with notices and food box, nobody showed up.

Then, one early morning after the storm, Jules was watching the bedraggled little coyote through his binoculars. It was on the other side of the teeming river. Suddenly, he thought he saw arms reaching up out of the water just where the swollen rivulet joined the rapid flow of the river. He had to investigate. So, with horror in his mind, he tramped through the squelching mud and downpour of rain to get a closer look. He was relieved to find that it was only a parka that seemed to have been swept down the rivulet and been caught on a willow branch.

When he told Hana, they decided they ought to go and look at the hillside. If the children were hiding up there one of them could be in a lot of trouble without a parka after so many cold nights and so much rain. Though it was incredibly dangerous to cross that swollen river, they went, prepared with thick strong ropes, blankets and first aid things, and food in case they found children in trouble. They got across by lassoing the rope to a stump on the other side, then using it to cling to as they hauled themselves and their backpack across. Swimming was impossible in that force of water. They reached the other side as drowned-looking and bedraggled as the wet coyote, and shook themselves like dogs, wringing the worst wet out of their jeans and jackets before they started the search and climb. "Better keep moving to get warm," Jules said through shivering teeth as they began to slip and climb up the hillside.

The little coyote ran up ahead of them, stopping again and again to make small snapping noises, like conversation. "Where've you been, little one?" Hana called to it softly. "We haven't seen much of you lately."

When the coyote was a very small puppy, they had found it whimpering in a hole in the hillside, apparently abandoned. After a while, when no parents showed up to rescue the poor little thing, Hana and Jules had taken it home and given it a box under their balcony and fed it. They hadn't tried to make it into a pet. It was a wild thing and they wanted to be sure it would be independent enough to survive. It was the little coyote that led them to Jasmin's hiding-hollow, quite near the place where they had first found the abandoned puppy.

When they found Jasmin, they were both soaked and shivering. They could tell she was ill; she acted strange and confused, her eyes wild and almost filled up with bright blue pupils, her cheeks gaunt and feverish.

They saw the only thing to do was to move her and her possessions into their home, so they packed everything carefully, then steered her down the slippery, squelching hillside to the river, trying between them to keep her warm with her quilt. Wildly, she insisted on wearing an old straw hat, fought them with some strange determined strength if they tried to carry it for her.

When they got her home, dried off, wrapped in a brown dressing gown and tucked under a blanket by the open fireplace, they talked in whispers so as not to wake her from the deep sleep she had fallen into.

"I think she's all right," Hana said as she laid a hand on Jasmin's damp forehead. "A bit feverish from weakness, I should think. She's very thin."

"Weakness!" Jules exclaimed. "I thought she was going to pull us both under the way she fought us."

Hana nodded wisely. "The strength of desperation. I don't think she wanted to be rescued. I think she liked it in that den—the way she had her things arranged."

"Kinda funny—that long red gown, Hana."

"Kinda beautiful." Hana smiled, looking at Jasmin. "This is definitely the girl in the photo. The boy must have had his own den, there was no sign of him in that one."

"I'll get going and find him," Jules said confidently.

"I ought to come with you for safety's sake but I can't very well leave this one—" Hana fretted.

"I'll be careful," he promised as he went.

He was away a long time, but returned empty-handed having found no trace of Leroy.

Jasmin's eyelashes were fluttering, warning Jules and Hana that she was coming awake.

Jules whispered very quietly, "Not a sign of

the boy. Not a thing to suggest he's been anywhere near there at all."

"Shh," Hana warned him. "Don't mention the brother for a bit. You never know—perhaps something terrible—he was retarded. Let's go easy on that. Play it by ear. See what information this one volunteers when she wakes."

26

JASMIN COULD FEEL HERSELF WAKING, EMERGING mixed up from the blackness of her sleep. She heard her own voice trying to yell, "Go away. Go away." Something was wrong with her head. She sat up and tried to hold it together because it felt as if it was breaking up and shooting out pieces like fireworks.

"Oh, go away. Please go away. I don't want you to find me. Nobody's going to find me," she mumbled. When she opened her eyes she saw the faces watching her and she remembered they were THEM PEOPLE. But the faces changed into flames, flames getting nearer and nearer. She closed her eyes quickly. That was awful. She felt as if she was on a swing, going up very high then falling, falling, while the ground rolled all around her. She opened her eyes and saw the flames going away smaller and smaller until they were in a little box like TV. Then the flames came rushing at her again, bigger and bigger and her head seemed to get bigger and bigger with the two faces pushing into it with the flames.

"Oh, please go away, leave me alone," she called out as the faces and the flames burst into her head again.

She tried to hold her head still between her hands, like holding a camera, so she could keep the pictures still. For a brief moment her eyes focused on the fireplace where flames were licking round a big log. She saw the man and the woman in a room that wasn't her hiding-hollow. Then she closed her eyes and immediately felt as if she was on a swing again, going so high she was sailing right over the top while the ground underneath was rocking and turning.

"Shhh, go steady, little one." A low voice was soothing her and a cool hand was put gently on her forehead.

Little one—that wasn't right, her confused head tried to say. Another voice was saying, "It's okay, little lady, hold on. It's okay, little lady."

Little lady—that wasn't right either. As the fireworks broke again behind her eyes she managed to say almost clearly, "I'm the oldest. Please leave me alone. I don't need you."

Jules and Hana looked at each other with a look that said, Now what do we do? They weren't used to dealing with young girls.

Hana tried to reason gently, "But, you had no clothes." Before she could say anything else Jasmin broke in angrily. "I would have made some. I didn't need you. I didn't need rescuing." She looked very odd as she was arguing because she had to hold her head to keep Jules' and Hana's faces in focus. Even before she finished speaking she had to put her head down between her knees because of another burst of fireworks, but not before she had seen her clay animals arranged on the stone hearth in front of the fire beside a mug of milk that was steaming next to a plate with a chunky piece of fruit bread with yellow butter on it. Next to that was the gold edge of her thin book reflecting the fire's flames. She heard her voice breaking out harshly with rude words that she could not stop. "You'd no business to meddle with my things. They're mine." Words she couldn't control lashed out at the two concerned faces, "You had no business to meddle where you didn't belong. Those things are mine. They're mine," she shouted. "And I don't need your food."

"We know, we know," Jules tried to soothe her. "They're mighty fine things, little lady." That "little lady" didn't sound right to Jasmin. Even through the confusion of her crazy head it didn't sound like the sort of thing a Dandron person would say. She moved her head from side to side trying to get herself and everything that was happening to her straight while the other voice, Hana's soft husky voice, was explaining, "We didn't mean to meddle, really we didn't. We thought you needed help. The rain still doesn't look as though it intends to stop."

And Jules added, "There's not much food for the picking in this weather."

That remark made Jasmin put her chin out proudly and assert, "Yes, there is. There's always something in the outdoors. There's mushrooms and there's berries." Then she had to screw up her eyes and dip her head down again. It made her mad that her head was behaving so strangely and she couldn't stop it.

Jules and Hana both lifted their shoulders in a little shrug to each other and Hana put her cool hand on Jasmin's forehead again and murmured, "Honey, sip a little warm sweet milk and you'll feel better. You're weak."

Jasmin couldn't resist, even though she wanted to. She lifted her head and gulped at the milk that was sweetened with honey.

"Just the stuff to fix up a rumbling tummy," Jules chuckled.

"Don't you dare laugh at me," Jasmin heard that rude voice of hers daring to shout. She might have yelled more rude things but the fireworks crashed and burst again out of her eyes.

"Nobody's laughing, honey," Hana assured her. "That's right, drink a little more—slowly. Your wild food on an empty stomach, then the cold river—well, they've all made you pretty woozy."

"Just calm down, little lady. You'll soon be fine again, then we can talk." Jules spoke matter-of-factly. "Nobody is going to know anything about you. Nobody is even going to know you are here. We don't have a telephone. The rivers are in full flood, the bridges all out, and the roads impassable. So relax. As soon as you feel better and calmer we can talk sensibly and decide what is to be done."

"That's the way it is, kid," Hana spoke sharply

and wagged her finger at Jasmin when she opened
her mouth to argue defiantly again, but her green
eyes were kind in her freckled face. "Take a breath
and listen. I'm Hana."

"And I'm Jules."

Hana wagged her finger again and said, "Now
be polite. Tell us your name."

Jasmin held her head between her hands and
looked hopelessly at the two pairs of eyes smiling
down at her. Did she have any choice? She sighed
and told them. "Jasmin."

"That's a pretty name." Jules smiled.

Jasmin grunted. It was the first time she had
ever heard anybody, apart from her mother, say it
was pretty. "Umph, you haven't heard the rest,"
she said.

"Well, tell us," they both said.

For a moment Jasmin let go her head, just long
enough to lift her chin, screw up her nose and ask,
"Would you believe—Jasmin Marie Antoinette
Stalke?"

"I'd believe. Nothing wrong with that," Jules
assured her.

"Name fit for a princess." Hana supported him.

"Or for a queen," added Jules.

"You got to be kidding," Jasmin muttered
unbelievingly, and as she spoke managed to stand up
and shed her blanket. But she had to flop down
quickly in a nearby chair, a pale wooden rocking
chair. "How did you know to say that?" she asked
suspiciously. "That's what my mother says. You
haven't been talking to my mother, have you?"

"No—no." Jules sounded surprised. "I mean it. You've got a pretty nice name there."

"But, I bet your mother is worried," Hana said quickly. Jasmin immediately held her head because of the flashing in it and cried out, "Don't tell her I'm here. I can't go back, ever, so don't tell her. I'm never going back so don't you dare tell anybody you saw me. Please, please!" With that she sank back exhausted in the rocking chair, her eyes closed. Almost immediately she seemed to have fallen off to sleep again.

"What're we going to do?" Hana whispered as Jasmin's head fell forward. "She never mentioned the boy."

Jules whispered back, "I noticed. I'll have another look round. I'll feed the fawn on the way."

Hana and Jules nodded to each other. He went out again to look for signs of Leroy while Hana sat in another rocking chair opposite Jasmin, while flames licked at the big log and the rain hissed down steadily, blurring the windows.

27

EGLANTINE AND MERRON DAMION HUGH HAD BOTH caught colds from getting wet so often. They were lying one at each end of the purple chesterfield sharing a gray blanket. The smell of the Vicks ointment that Olive had rubbed on their chests filled the room.

Every so often Olive noticed the piled-up dirty dishes by the tin bowl under the mirror, and the bits and pieces of half-eaten snacks all over the table, and the mud tracked all over the floor, and new tears flowed down her cheeks as she moaned, "This house do sure miss Jasmin. My Jasmin, such a big help to her mother. Such a good girl."

Honey Angelina was fretful all the time and the TV was turned up loud. The same old news was cheerfully announced again and again with news flashes of flooded basements and roads like rivers adding excitement to the words about disaster and thousands of dollars in property damages.

One newsman, jolly as a Santa Claus, boomed out that the news was good. "Fine weather on the way. Sunshine forecast for tomorrow." He had to hurry his words up to get them in before the next commercial break. "As soon as visibility improves an intensivesearchwillbe resumedforthetwo childrenmissing fromthe districtwestofDandron." He gasped for breath. He was managing to get it all in in time. "Phew! Some storm, folks. Sure glad I wasn't caught out in that storm—yes sirree."

"Ah, shut yer silly city fat face, willya," Bud Stalke sneered at the announcer. He was tired and his shoulders drooped. He had been out searching every daylight hour, continually getting soaked through, Sam, his mighty horse, slipping and sliding on the water-soaked earth.

"City slicker like you 'ud be drownded in the first half hour. I'd throw you in the river if I had you here." Bud stormed over to the refrigerator as he roared at the TV and the big kids knew to keep out of his way.

But Marigold Lolita May was too young to understand. She put her dark little face out from under the table to ask, "Dad, Dad, is Jasmin and Leroy drownded?"

Bud made as though to reach down and hit her but stopped himself just in time. "Oh shut up, kid, willya. Don't you know any better," he cried out.

"Oh, my lovey, don't say things like that," Olive whimpered. "Oh, don't ever say such a thing. My Jasmin and Leroy aren't drownded. They're all right, I tell you. I knows they are alive somewhere. I tell you, I can feel it in my bones." Her body shuddered as more sobs burst out of her.

"Oh, for shucks sake, snap out of it, Olive," Bud nagged her in exasperation. "Instead of bawling why don't you tell me what a hungry man can put in his belly? Why don't yer get up off your big fat behind and get us a meal before we all snuff it from starvation. Bawling ain' going to do none of us no good. Sure ain't going to bring them kids back."

The cheery newscaster said that some bridges had already been repaired. "Holiday's nearly over, you kids out there. Could be school again, sooner than you think, kiddies."

"Better than this miserable house," Nathaniel muttered to himself.

Olive exploded into sobs again. "They've been gone such a long time. The longest six days in my life," she cried.

28

JASMIN WAS WAKING UP WITH THE SURE FEELING that something was wrong. She opened her eyes a fraction, saw her body wrapped tightly in a brown dressing gown, and felt her bare feet on the tufts of a hearth rug. She remembered where she was. She was sitting in a straight-backed rocking chair in the house of the meddling people who had rescued her. The rug was honey-colored. Oh yes, she remembered, they had been trying to humor her. Jules and Hana, THEM PEOPLE, they were trying to be nice to her, treating her like a little kid so she would go back to her family. But her head was still behaving strangely. She opened her eyes a bit wider to see if she could get things in focus without fireworks bursting. She didn't move in case THEM PEOPLE were looking at her, waiting to start humoring her again, talking to her carefully as though she were a little kid. She had to think what to do. They would never be able to understand her problems. They were just sorry for her poor mother. They would think she was selfish and hateful and crazy because she wanted to live *as she did please*.

Her head was feeling steadier but, without moving it, she moved her eyes round to see what she could see. At the other side of the rug, across from her, there was a pair of bare feet next to a flat wooden box of pastel crayons. A long brown skirt hung in folds around the legs. Hana's legs. A grownup with bare feet and crayons! Jasmin didn't know what to think about that. She could almost hear her father's voice saying sneeringly, "Bums, that's what they are. Living back there and never doing a day's work."

The log in the fireplace was crackling quietly and the rain outside was thudding on the ground. The room smelled like newly cut pine wood and the hearth where her animals were set out was made of brown, stripy rocks like the inside of her hiding-hollow. Books on shelves reached down to the floor on either side of the fireplace, some of them hidden behind Jasmin's red gown, which was on a coat-hanger hooked over an upper shelf. Jasmin had forgotten about not being ready to talk and lifted her head.

"It's a beautiful gown," Hana said. "I washed it carefully."

Jasmin said nothing but gradually turned her head to look at Hana, who was holding a drawing board upright on her knee with one hand and sketching with the other. Her braids were undone so her crinkled red hair hung down loosely. She had freckles on her brown hands.

"What are you looking at me for?" Jasmin heard her own voice ask rudely. She wasn't trying to be rude. It just came out that way.

155

Hana's reddish eyebrows shot up in surprise, and she answered quite sharply, "I guess a cat can look at a queen!" Then she added more gently, "I'm sketching. I make portraits and I thought I might as well do one of you while you're here."

"But I'm not staying," was the reply that burst out of Jasmin before she could think of anything else.

"All the more reason then for me to work quickly," Hana said and went on sketching. After a pause, while Jasmin held her head and didn't know what to say, Hana went on, speaking with pauses between her words while she narrowed her eyes to look at Jasmin, then opened them to look at what her fingers were drawing, "I thought I—might get—a portrait of you—lovely portrait—in your—red gown—"

Jasmin could hardly believe it. Why would anybody want a portrait of her? She figured she was being humored again. She kept quiet because she didn't know what to say but Hana eventually broke the silence again.

"I thought—I might use you for—a new portrait —and show—it—at the Witchitt Art and Science Fair next week."

Jasmin, not believing her ears, leaped to her feet tugging the brown dressing gown tightly around her. Her eyes wild and her chin thrusting out fiercely, she cried, "Oh no! No. You can't do that. You can't put a picture of me in Witchitt. Never. Never!"

Hana stopped, putting her drawing-board down flat on her knee, looked at Jasmin with surprise in her wide green eyes. "Okay kid. You don't have to shout at me. Calm down, eh. Nobody's going to do anything you don't want. Sit down. You look fierce as a raging lion. You scare me," she finished with a little laugh.

Jasmin had to sit down anyhow because of the fireworks in her head. She held it in her hands and sheepishly tried to explain without being rude, "I meant you can't put a picture of me in the Witchitt Fair because if you do everybody will know where I am. I don't want anybody to know where I am. I can't go back. I can't ever go back."

"Okay, okay. Stay calm. I have a portrait of Jules I can show. But I'd still like to do one of you, if you don't mind."

Jasmin only said grumpily, "It isn't an Art Fair. It's a Science Fair. They have it every year."

Hana had propped up her board and gone on sketching. "This year it's an Art Fair as well— Witchitt Art and Science Fair. Your information is out of date."

Jasmin sounded as though she wanted to argue when she mumbled, "It's always been a Science Fair."

"Things change, you know, even in Witchitt. We live in this district. We are artists, and—you've got nice long fingers—and—we're going to put some of our stuff in the fair—next week."

Jasmin felt self-conscious about her hands because Hana had mentioned them. She took them away from her head and folded her arms so her hands were hidden.

Hana looked away from her sketching and away from Jasmin to the clay animals on the hearth. Jasmin followed her gaze. They were paler now than when they had been in the hiding-hollow with her because they had dried, except the spruce grouse with the fanned out tail and the complicated one of the cougar and the doe. Somebody had put each one of those two in small clear plastic bags.

"Jules was very careful with them," Hana said. "We wondered if perhaps you were making them for the Fair."

"Why?" Again, Jasmin heard her voice sound impatient and rude. She didn't know what to say.

"Why?" Hana echoed. "Why? Because they're good, that's why. People would like to see them."

During that bit of conversation Jules had slipped quietly into the room, rubbing his hair with a big blue towel. "You can say that again," he joined in. "They *are* good and people *would* like to see them."

Jasmin stared down at the little clay animals on the hearth. Had she really made them? Suddenly it all seemed long ago that her fingers had what seemed like a magic power.

"Did you make them, Jasmin?" Jules asked.

Silly question, Jasmin thought. Who did he think had made them? "Sure, I did." She shrugged.

"Fine work." Jules sat on the edge of the hearth with the towel round his head and picked up the complicated cougar-doe, slipping it out of its bag with careful fingers and setting it on the palm of his big hand. "Quite a piece of work," he said quietly.

Jasmin looked at it there on his hand and remembered how difficult it had been to sort out. It looked so simple.

"Did you see this happen?" Jules nodded his head slightly toward the cougar and doe.

She didn't answer. She still felt trapped. These people would be nice to her and try to persuade her to go back to *failing*. She stared past Jules and his outstretched hand, at the red log in the fire.

Jules didn't wait for an answer but went on to say, "I was asking because, just before the storm broke, a fawn wandered up to our shed."

At the mention of the fawn, Jasmin lifted her face to look into the two faces that were looking at her with so much concern. The fawn! The poor thing left alone when the cougar dragged its mother away and the helicopter roared over the river.

"I just fed it," Jules said. "We have to give it a bottle."

Hana spoke quietly to say, "We don't know if it will survive. You have to be so careful not to make wild things tame, or they will never survive in the wilderness."

Jasmin felt her heart do a little dance of relief. The orphaned fawn was safe. That was a nice thing. She smiled.

Hana knelt down by the hearth and picked up the sculpture of the curled coyote. "This one seems to be surviving," she said. "We fed it when it was an abandoned pup."

Jasmin still said nothing. She rocked and rocked gently, her bare feet on the warm tufted rug. A lot of things were coming together in her head and she was surprised to find a little feeling of confidence now toward Hana and Jules.

Jules looked up to one of the windows. "The sky seems to be brightening," he said. "Looks as if the rain is finally coming to an end, and none too soon."

"Then I can go back to my hiding-hollow," Jasmin said quickly, and she saw an anxious glance pass between Jules and Hana.

Hana stood up and frowned. "Well, you can't go back yet," she said. "I had to wash your quilt. It was muddy and it smelled. You'll have to wait till it's dry."

Jasmin frowned and put her chin out, knowing Hana was just making an excuse. Again she saw the puzzled glance between Hana and Jules.

Jules asked her, "But what are we going to say to the police? Or to your parents? People are bound to come searching here. The Royal Canadian Mounted Police have already been here once."

"Please, can't you pretend you've never seen me because I'm never going back home again. I'm never going to school again. You've got to let me go back to my hiding-hollow. You've got to—please." Jasmin sounded desperate but determined.

Jules argued with her, saying, "Look, Jasmin,

even if we fit you out with clothes and bedding, even with a supply of food—how could you survive in winter?"

"I would survive. I know I could survive."

Hana shook her head. "Jasmin, Jasmin," she pleaded. "You can't live in a coyote den forever."

Jasmin answered her fiercely. "When everybody is sure I'm dead, then I can move further into the mountains and find a shack. There are empty shacks. I could fix it up."

"This conversation's getting us nowhere, Jasmin," Jules said firmly. "We know where you are. We can't lie to people who care about you. Why don't you tell us what you're running away from?"

Hana nodded in support. "Yes, maybe we can help you."

Jasmin dug her toes into the rug and looked at her bony knees making mountains in the brown dressing gown. "Nobody can help me," she said. "It's hopeless." But even as she said it she was thinking how nice it would be to tell somebody about *failing*. Perhaps it would be all right to tell these two, she thought. If they know about leaving wild animals free so they can survive, perhaps they would understand about leaving her free so she could survive. She looked round the room while she was making up her mind, out of the windows that looked through dripping trees down the misty valley of the river. She looked round the walls, the pale, piney log walls. Her eyes rested on three large pictures of birds on the wall opposite her. They made her take a sharp breath, made her forget her problems and she stood up to look at them more close up. They gave her the free feeling, the dance-y feeling she got when she'd just finished a sculpture.

"I'm going to show those at the Witchitt Fair," Jules told her quietly. Jasmin didn't react to the mention of Witchitt and the Fair, she was so caught and held by the spell the paintings held for her. They were a surprise that kept on being a surprise. She stood there with her mouth open. One was a painting of a vivid bluejay flying and flashing in a surge of color and freedom. In another, red-capped woodpeckers climbed vertically up the strong silver lines of a white poplar trunk. The pattern of lines seemed to make the hammering sound of wood-peckers pecking in the clean air. The third picture was a merry design of winter-bare branches alive with the fat round bodies of a flock of mountain chickadees, bodies like sharp little notes of music. Jasmin smiled, then laughed out loud.

"I wish I could make pictures like that," she said.

"Well, I wouldn't be surprised if you could," Jules answered her seriously. "I wish I could make sculptures like yours."

"I wouldn't be surprised if you could," said Jasmin and turned round to sit down and to smile at the two gentle people. She thought maybe she could trust them. They seemed to care about the same sort of things that she had found out she cared about. She put her chin out. She had decided to tell about her problems.

Quietly she told them about the too-much homework, the too-many children, the ruined science project, and the certainty of *failing*.

29

SHE DID HOPE THAT JULES AND HANA WEREN'T TRICKING her because she told them so many of her private thoughts and secrets as well as her troubles. It ended up being one of the cosiest days she had ever had. It was almost as perfect as the best day in her hiding-hollow. She didn't have to do anything. She sat on the rug by the fire sipping mugs of creamy hot chocolate, eating cinnamon toast and apples and dates and nuts. It was the first time in her life she could remember being waited on. It was nice, for a change. Hana sketched, Jules played with a piece of clay making the figure of a girl with long hair sitting with her legs curled round. "You've made me want to see what I can do with the rough clay around here," he told Jasmin. She just sat talking. But Jules and Hana talked, too, sharing their ideas with her so she began to feel like a friend instead of the girl they thought they were rescuing. They told her how it was their dream come true, to be living in the wilderness in a house they had built by themselves.

Sometimes though, Jasmin knew that Jules and Hana exchanged a secret look. There was something they weren't telling her. There was some question they weren't asking her, she could tell.

"Did you tell Leroy you were mad at him when he ruined your Fair project?" Hana asked.

"No," Jasmin answered, "you don't have to tell Leroy when you're mad. He just knows." As she said it she saw a glance pass between Hana and Jules.

"Leroy must know then that you were terribly upset," Jules conjectured quietly as he made texture on the hair of the clay model with his thumbnail and then held it at arms length to look at it while Jasmin answered.

"He would be the only one in the world who knew," she said and felt tears sting her eyes as she thought of poor, big, gentle Leroy. She put out her chin to stop her own gentle feelings, because she had to be tough. "Now you two know," she ended, and hoped again that they were not tricking her. Hana's next question made it sound as though they might be.

"Would you stop your running away if you could prove you have enough brains to pass your grade?"

Jasmin made her eyes hard and kept her chin out. "I don't stand a chance," she said with finality, but added when neither Jules nor Hana said anything, "Anyhow, I like living by myself. You've got to let me go back to my hiding-hollow, or somewhere—to live as I do please—like—*Old Meg*." Jasmin nodded toward her poetry book. She had even told these people about her secret treasure and the crowded attic. Why had she told them everything?

Quickly she put on an *I don't care face,* to be ready if they laughed at her or showed it was all a trick.

Jules did laugh. He chuckled. Jasmin stared at him with her eyes gone hard.

"Oh, Jasmin, you dreamer, has it never occurred to you that Old Meg was just a poet's dream? The young man who wrote about that wild, proud Meg ended coughing up blood, dying slowly in a small room in a big city. Didn't you know?"

"Did he die?" Jasmin asked, surprised.

"Before he was as old as me, or Hana."

"How old?"

"Twenty-five. Perhaps *to live as he did please* was his hopeless dream."

"Well, you two live as you do please, don't you?"

"Almost," Hana joined in.

"We have ways of making a living—ways we like—but we've worked very hard."

"We both stuck it out at school."

There it was, just as she expected, they were going to preach at her to go back to school. Jasmin almost sounded rude again as she asked, "How can you make a living in this place?"

Jules and Hana both laughed.

"We sometimes wonder," Hana said.

"Just a little tiny living, that's all," Jules added with a laugh. "Hana is an illustrator. She's done a few children's books."

"And Jules is a naturalist, a photographer, a painter, a Jack-of-all-trades when needs arise. Luckily our needs are simple."

"I wouldn't mind living like you do—*as you do please*," Jasmin said ruefully.

"Maybe you could," Jules said matter-of-factly. "You seem to have a lot of talent in those fingers. Maybe you could go on to get trained and qualified to make good use of it."

Jasmin only grunted. What was the use? She couldn't even pass into junior high school.

Hana seemed to read her thoughts. She said, making the suggestion very carefully, "Perhaps you could use your clay animals as part of a science project. There's a lot of work gone into them. You could make a sort of wilderness habitat in a box and put them in it—if you wanted to."

"In a cardboard box? A big one," Jasmin asked with a funny feeling because she was remembering her nightmare about taking a big cardboard box into the Witchitt Arena and searching for her name.

"Sure. Take the side out of the box."

"Paint it first," Jules added.

"There's lots of paint in the studio upstairs," Hana said.

"There's glue and any amount of stuff you might find useful and you're welcome to use anything we've got."

"Sounds like fun," said Jules.

It did sound like fun, Jasmin thought, when those two were talking. She got caught up in their enthusiasm and began to see it happening in her head. "I could build up a landscape with earth and clay and pine needles. Stick pieces of branches in for

166

trees. There are broken bits everywhere after the storm. Make a river through it." She was getting excited when a thought suddenly struck her. "But I bet my teachers would say it wasn't science."

"No, they wouldn't. The environment is science," Jules said with certainty.

"Well," Hana put in a small warning. "It would only be science if you did it really well. I think you could."

"Your animals are well observed."

"And maybe you've inherited your grandmother's skill and patience for details.

"I hope so," Jasmin said and looked at her thin fingers. Perhaps they were like her grandmother's, and a little hope began to grow in her. Perhaps she could get a science project done. "But a wilderness habitat wouldn't prove to my teachers that I've got enough brains to spell and make charts and pass my grade, would it?" she asked with a new uncertainty.

"It would to me," Jules said firmly.

"But you're special," Jasmin blurted out, then felt silly for saying such a thing. Jules just smiled.

"We think you're pretty special too, kid," Hana said quickly so as not to sound soppy. "We're glad we found you. But I do think we should try to work out a way for you to make going home again a possibility."

Jules supported what she was saying. "Yes, Jasmin, give the wilderness habitat a try for starters, will you?"

"Okay," Jasmin agreed but slowly as though she might just start being argumentative again about living alone.

Hana put an end to that. She yawned and said, "Let that be enough decisions for tonight. Bedtime. Let me show you."

Jasmin had to sleep on a couch in the studio that was up a staircase. The big room was full of windows that let in the star-filled sky and it smelled of paints. Jasmin liked the smell.

"You'll have to put up with the mess," Hana said, "but I'll put up a screen to shut you off in your own small corner."

To Jasmin it was beautiful. For the second time in her life she felt as if she had a special place of her own. She was soon sleeping peacefully.

30

IT WAS ANOTHER LOVELY WAKING UP; FIRST THE smell of artist's paints and papers and the piney fragrance of the house itself, then the bright, soft morning sunshine falling in the eastern windows. Jasmin took in a contented breath, wriggled her toes and stretched her legs and studied the screen by her couch side. It was made of cloth stretched across three wooden arches that had been hinged together. The way the cloth had been dyed seemed like magic.

It gave the idea of a forest of many greens with blue birds and yellow birds flashing among them. Somehow it was just the feel of an idea, like when she had awakened in the forest to look up at the undersides of birds and squirrels, up to the bright patterns of blue sky.

Jasmin found herself thinking that maybe, if she ever went back home, she could make a screen for her bedside in the attic. If she ever went home! Why had she even thought of that? She was not going home, was she?

But she had sort of promised Hana and Jules that she would give the wilderness habitat idea a try. So, she got up and saw the mist lying low all down the valley with the sun sometimes breaking through in shafts like morning pathways of gold. She saw too that clothes had been put out for her on a stool at the bottom of the couch. They were a bit big she found as she got into them. She had to roll up the jeans. The blue knitted sweater was baggy and the thick blue socks too big—but it didn't matter, did it?

Jules and Hana had thought of everything. On the long table in the studio, next to a big cardboard box, there was a knife for hacking the front off and to make the sides the rough, natural sort of hilly shape that she wanted. There were scissors, tubes of paint and saucers for mixing it in. There were plastic pails for collecting the stuff from outside. Jasmin took them and, moving silently on sock feet through the silent house, she crept out. She didn't want anybody to wake until her work was done. And she wanted to do it well. She wanted Hana and Jules to go on believing she could make marvelous things.

She crept down the stairs and found boots had been put out for her. Outside the mist lay wet on her hair and eyelashes. The river rushed and roared. Everywhere chirps and whistles told her that the forest was waking. It was early. She had time.

She filled plastic pails with clay and lighter earth, with pine needles, little clumps of grass, broken-off bits of branch, pebbles, pinecones, mosses. Soon, she was back in the studio working at making the world of her hiding-hollow in the big cardboard box. She hacked the box sides into uneven shapes, then with clay and earth molded the slope and contours of her hillside. With pebbles and thin slivers of foil she made it seem that the rivulet of water was gurgling down the gully. Joyfully she made her hiding-hollow and found just the right curved piece of jackpine twig to make it the way it was, with a curtain of green needles spreading down to make the place secret. The dance-y feeling was filling her mind and body again as her fingers worked swiftly and well.

She knew exactly where she wanted to put each one of her animals. The moose was to stand in tall grasses because she was not going to put the big river in. As she spread the twig-trees and old pine needles she could feel as though she was there among them, small, in her own place, making her larder safe in the gully, picking mushrooms. She painted all the cardboard box, even the back of it, so it didn't look as though it had ever been just an old brown box. It was transformed into a wilderness habitat. At last, when she stood back to look at it, thinking it might be done, she felt like singing. As she cleaned up her mess, she kept taking satisfied looks at her handiwork.

"Is it okay if we come up?" Hana called up the stairs.

"Now, I like that. That's pretty good," Jules said slowly and thoughtfully as he stood back to get an overall view of her wilderness habitat.

Hana gave Jasmin a little hug and Jules went downstairs to bring up the animals. The three of them arranged them in their places, standing back again and again to see how splendid and convincing the whole thing looked.

"We'll have to spray the pine needles with some gluey stuff to keep the surface in place," Jules said. "And we'll take the sculptures out and wrap them separately. They have to be treated gently so they don't get chipped or broken. You can put them in place there."

There! That meant at the Witchitt Fair.

Jasmin looked down at her floppy big socks. It was one thing to make the habitat to please Hana and Jules but it was a different matter to think of *going back*. Even with a science project, she would feel so silly.

Hana seemed to read her thoughts. She said, "You wouldn't feel too badly. All the kids have missed some school because of the storm."

Jasmin said nothing. The dance-y feeling had gone.

"Well, I'm hungry. Let's eat," said Jules. Jasmin knew he was trying to pass over the awkward moment.

Downstairs she saw that her quilt was neatly folded on the hearth with her red gown on top of it, and on top of that her poetry book. It looked so final. Next to that pile there was another with red and brown sneakers, some folded socks, a small pile of underwear and a brown-blanket jacket. Everything was ready for her to leave. She looked at the two piles in despair. She wished desperately, in that moment, that she could dash away back to her dear hiding-hollow or better still that, as in a fairy tale or a TV show, Hana and Jules would say she could live with them so they could all live happily ever after. But it wasn't a fairy story or TV for Jasmin Stalke, she knew that. She stuck out her chin and sat down to breakfast.

For a while they ate silently, thick fruit bread with honey. It was good. But now it seemed that Jules and Hana and Jasmin didn't know what to say to each other. They all kept looking out the window into the misty valley. Jasmin felt that Jules and Hana wanted to tell her something. They didn't say anything though until the sun suddenly broke through the mist to show a clear view down the valley. Then Hana broke the silence. "When the mist clears, they'll be out looking for you."

"What are we to do, Jasmin?" Jules asked and waited for her to look him in the eye. "Now, before you answer, we have a few things to tell you, or ask you. So just listen."

"First," Hana carried on, "sometimes we would

like to go away for a few days. We could use a sort of baby-sitter for the house. Could we offer you the job? You really don't live so far away."

Then Jules went on without waiting for Jasmin to answer. "And we thought that perhaps, some weekends, when your mother doesn't need you to help, you could come down here and we could do some more work with clay—or things."

"You might even catch up with your homework then."

Jasmin spread honey thickly on another slice of bread. She knew exactly how they were trying to make it easy for her to go home. She was very grateful for their kindness. But it was impossible to think of going home. She couldn't make her mind face up to it. She just wanted to go on running away and running away. She would feel so silly going home.

"But we have something else, something more serious, much more serious to tell you."

"What?" Jasmin heard her voice lash out sharply. She had known all the time there was something they weren't telling her. "What?" she repeated.

Jules said very quietly, "The searchers will not be looking just for you."

"Who else?" Jasmin asked with her eyes wide open and her breath standing still.

"Your brother. The one who follows you everywhere."

Jasmin's hand, with the honey-thick slice of bread in it, stopped dead in front of her open mouth. At that moment the sound of a distant helicopter rattled through the lifting mist. Hana and Jules looked anxiously at Jasmin who slowly put her bread down on the brown plate. She lifted her chin and crinkled her lips tightly. Her eyes went very bright with tears that she would not let fall. She let out a short angry sigh.

"Just because I wasn't there." She snorted a sigh of anger and despair. "There was nobody to look after him." Then she said to Hana and Jules as though trying to convince them that *she* hadn't been careless about him, "I did make sure he didn't follow me. Poor Leroy. Oh, poor Leroy."

Hana and Jules didn't know what to say. They just looked at her with sad and serious eyes.

The helicopter sounded nearer.

Inside her head Jasmin could just see Leroy with his pale eyes struggling to understand. No one to wipe his mouth and push his tongue in. She closed her eyes against the shaft of sunlight that spread down the honey golden table and she saw Marigold Lolita May with a dirty face, Merron Damion Hugh with his laces undone and his shoes on the wrong feet. She saw the messy table and dirty dishes piling up and she saw having to bathe for everybody to see on a Sunday night, the crowded attic, everything.

"Okay," she said softly and stood up slowly, tucking her chair in its place under the table. "I have to go back. I have to find Leroy." Her mind was made up. "We can wave to the helicopter when it searches around here."

"Okay," was all Jules and Hana said.

They packed her things in a soft traveling bag with their old labels on it. "You can let us have it back when you visit us again," Hana said and smiled.

Jules said to get in touch with them by leaving a note in their mailbox in the Dandron post office. "We can leave notes for you in the Stalke mailbox."

Jasmin felt they meant it, that they intended to be her friends. She wanted to say something special to them but she didn't know how without sounding soppy and silly. Instead she took her old poetry book from the top of the things in the traveling bag. "You can have this," was all she said.

While they were waiting for the helicopter to land, Jules promised he would take her science project to the Witchitt Fair.

Just before the helicopter got too loud for them to say any more, Hana shouted, "Is it okay now if I put your portrait in the show?"

"I guess," Jasmin agreed as the clacking blades turned the air into a swirl and rush. "It doesn't matter now."

"Good luck," they shouted as Jasmin was lifted away, *going back*.

31

THE HELICOPTER PILOT RADIOED THAT HE HAD LO-cated the girl and was picking her up. He reported that she was in excellent condition.

The Royal Canadian Mounted Police phoned the Stalke house to tell them the girl would be delivered in the open field just across the road from their place and that a member of the force would be there almost immediately to get particulars.

Bud Stalke was just getting up when the phone rang.

"Oli, Oli, d'ye hear that; they've got the phones fixed," he called. But when he listened to the message he was too confused to collect his ideas and ask questions. He passed the message on to all the family just as the voice had told it to him, "She will be put down, home safe, in just the time it will take you to get across the road to meet her." Immediately, all the family rushed out as they were; some half dressed, some in their nightclothes, they all rushed out and left the TV shouting to itself. They rushed out, running through the upturned cars and old machinery, toward the road.

Up above in the mist-washed blue morning sky Jasmin was murmuring over and over to herself, "Poor Leroy, oh poor Leroy." At first the helicopter pilot turned to her with a cheerful smile and jolly questions. He must have thought she was stupid or something because she only looked at him with empty eyes and did not seem to be rejoicing at all that she was being rescued. Her mind was shivering and falling into caves of black horror as it said over and over, "Poor Leroy, poor Leroy."

Down below she saw the whirring shadow of the helicopter blades on the bushland where the trees looked like soft green cushions. It looked so safe and happy down there, rivers and roads making sharp twisting patterns. The world down there seemed like a toy one with small houses. How would she find Leroy in all that? The fields showed the patterns where tractors had gone round and round. Would Leroy show up on such perfect patterns? Jasmin peered down at the earth, eager to believe that somewhere she would see Leroy's white head and flailing arms.

The helicopter floated lower. The soft green cushions changed to spiky trees. There! The pilot pointed out the Stalke house and she saw the family running through the junk, everybody looking up and waving to the sky.

But what would she say to them? Her stomach went queasy at the thought. What would they say to her? Would her father hit her round the ears because she had driven him wild? Would her mother shout at her? Would all the kids hate her because she had lost Leroy? Oh, how could she bear it? She felt dizzy with fear and embarrassment.

Her father leaped over the fence. All the kids were crawling underneath. Her mother was squeezing between the strands of barbed wire while her father held them. Eglantine was holding Honey Angelina. They were all waving and running. Then they were bending their heads as people do on TV when they run up to a helicopter. Then somehow her father was swinging her down to the ground and hugging her, and everybody was looking at her and saying excitedly, "Jasmin. Jasmin." She didn't have to say anything. Her mother hugged her and squeezed her against her big soft body then stroked her hair and sobbed, "Oh, Jasmin, Jasmin, we was thinking we should never see you again." The little kids were hugging her legs.

The helicopter pilot reminded Bud that the Royal Canadian Mounted Police would be at the house in no time to take a statement.

Bud picked up Jasmin's bag and the helicopter roared away. For a moment or two all was noise and confusion, then as it became quiet enough for them to hear each other, everybody seemed to say at the same moment, "But where's Leroy?"

Everybody stood still to look at Jasmin. "Leroy was never with me. I never saw him," she said and felt she wanted to die when she saw the horrified and hopeless looks on her mother's and father's faces. "I've come home to find him. I'll find him," Jasmin said quickly. But her mother had broken up into small screams and sobs, tears streaming off her face. The kids all looked solemn. Bud's thin shoulders drooped. He said, "Well, whatever, let's get inside and hear what you have to say." So they all got through the fence, crossed the gravel road, went in past the dead cars and junk stuff and into the hot room where the TV was singing.

Jasmin was back home.

Eglantine sat Honey Angelina down on the floor by the chesterfield, pushed her glasses up her nose and the first thing she said to Jasmin was, "Where did you get them clothes?"

Honey Angelina put her arms for Jasmin to pick her up, which she did and put her face in the

178

baby's soft warm hair to hide it from Bud's hopeless question, "So, Jasmin, you mean you never took Leroy with you?"

Then the two Mounties came in and sat straddling chairs they'd turned backwards. They began asking her questions. Everybody stood around to listen, her mother sobbing, her father with bent shoulders, Marigold Lolita May with a runny nose and wearing a dirty nightgown. Jasmin wished they weren't all standing there listening. How could she tell the big clean men with their polished shoes and shiny pink faces that she'd run away? Suddenly she felt very stubborn. How could she tell these men that she couldn't get her homework done? How could she tell them that there were too many children here? She felt very little and silly. But stubborn. She wasn't going to tell these strong and perfect men about *failing*.

"No, I never saw anybody until I went to the house after the storm."

Jasmin stuck her chin out and made her eyes go hard so they wouldn't think she wanted to cry. Jasmin Stalke never let anybody make her cry, she told herself fiercely.

"No, I never saw my brother.

"I got lost, that's all. It's easy to get lost in the forest.

"I was just going out for an adventure. I got lost.

"Yes, I'm sure there was never anybody with me.

"Yes, I was afraid sometimes.

"No. No. I don't know where Leroy is.

"I know I caused everybody a lot of worry. I said I'm sorry. I'm sorry."

Questions. Questions.

Stubborn answers with her chin out and her eyes hard. When the Mounties left they said the search for Leroy would be intensified because with one child alive there was some hope for the other.

Jasmin wanted to go out immediately to start her private search for Leroy but her father and mother both said that she'd better not go out by herself again—ever. Bud said she was to stay at home right where her mother could see her. He went off with a bunch of men to search some more.

Except for Leroy, it felt to Jasmin that she had never been away at all. She wiped off the table and cleaned up the dishes, all the time wondering and worrying about places Leroy might be. She tried to mop up some of the mud from the floor but only managed to spread it around. Her mother kept on crying and the TV kept shouting till Jasmin thought she would go crazy. The newscast announced that there would be school in the Dandron district to-morrow now the weather had changed and bridges were repaired. School? Oh school! How could she face it? But that wasn't as bad as Leroy. She kept making her mind focus on Leroy. She began to be-lieve that if she concentrated on him hard enough she could get a message to him. "Leroy, Jasmin's coming. Jasmin will find you."

She kept arguing with her mother and begging

to be allowed to go out to look for Leroy. "He'll come for me. You know he'll come for me."

"Oh, your father said I wasn't to let you out of my sight, Jasmin. We never thought you'd be the one to cause us trouble, you the oldest, the one we depend on." Then Olive cried some more.

But at last she gave in and said Jasmin could go so long as she took the other kids with her.

So in the heat of the late afternoon sun, Jasmin set off down the winding road with Eglantine, Nathaniel, Carmen Miranda Elisa and Merron Damion Hugh trailing along. They soon grew tired of searching. They trailed their hands in the long grasses, kicked pebbles, and asked Jasmin hundreds of little-kid questions which she answered with as much patience as she could find while her heart and mind were crying out across the hot, steaming landscape, "Leroy, oh Leroy, please let us find you."

32

WHEN SHE FOUND LEROY SHE WANTED TO BE SICK.

The others had urged her to turn back ages before. "It's time we went back home, before Mom gets too worried," Eglantine insisted. "You've already caused everybody enough worry without getting us all yelled at for being out too long. Anyhow, it's too hot. And I'm not going to carry Carmen any more. You can."

"And I've got a big blister on my heel," Nathaniel grumbled tiredly. "We ain't going to find Leroy. Eg and me've looked round here. Dad's looked down here. Everybody's searched down here."

Merron Damion Hugh had scratched the mosquito bites on his ankles and arms until he was bleeding.

"Okay," Jasmin agreed hopelessly. "But first, just let me look in the old house, then I'll carry Carmen and we'll go back."

"Ain't no good looking there. Just an old cat lives in there," Nathaniel told her. "Everybody's searched in there too. It stinks."

"We seen it," Eglantine said as though she was ready to die of heat. "Seen the wild cat. The Mounties said nobody would be in there with the stink and the wild cat—they said so—see. They searched it."

"Well, you guys stay in the shade and have a rest while I take a look," Jasmin ordered them.

"Ain't nothing in there," both Nathaniel and Eglantine called after her as she ran ahead to look in the derelict old house. Jasmin called Leroy's name at the window, softly but desperately.

Once inside, the smell struck her, even before her eyes got used to the dim light. It was cold in there. Cold and earthy. Like a tomb. She called his name again, softly. There was no answer, not the slightest sound. She could see now. It was creepy.

There were small corpses—dead animals—a gopher, three field mice, a small fat gray vole and a brown squirrel with big staring eyes. Even creepier, all the dead animals were hung over a broken floorboard that disappeared in the black hole underneath. The animals were carefully arranged on the long board with their heads all pointing the same way and their tails hanging over the other side. It was a larder. Jasmin knew it was a larder. The big black cat that Eglantine and Nathaniel had seen was bringing in food. But would a cat arrange the animals all the same way? Would it? Jasmin's instincts told her that this was something to do with Leroy. He loved little animals. Leroy had to be somewhere in this place.

She called again softly, "Leroy. Jasmin's here."

There was no sound except wasps buzzing shrilly in the cavity of a wall and the faraway voices of the other kids out in the sunshine. Jasmin shivered.

She lay down and peered through the hole in the broken floor. There didn't seem room for anybody to hide under there except spiders. Crawly spiders in milky thick webs. But she had to search thoroughly. She held her breath and squeezed down under the broken floor, watched by the dead eyes of the corpses. Their tails touched her cheek and spider webs breathed on her lips. She wiped them away and called softly, "Leroy, it's me. It's Jasmin."

It was even darker down there. This could once have been a pioneer root cellar where potatoes, carrots and things were stored. It smelled old and horrible. She couldn't bear to go any further, but she knew that Leroy was down there. It was worse than a nightmare—the terrible black hole was real. "Oh Leroy, come on out," she pleaded desperately. "Please come out. Come out for Jasmin."

There was no sound. Only her own breathing.

She called again, wheedling, pleading. She didn't want to crawl any further in that nightmare place. The kids' voices, faraway in the sunshine, sounded unreal. "Oh Leroy, please, please come out. I know you're there. I know. I know." How silly she'd feel if she cried now, but she was ready to cry. She began to crawl further in the dark hole. There was nothing else to do. "Leroy, it's me. It's Jasmin," she kept on calling gently.

Then she heard something. She heard muffled struggling sounds.

Her heart stood still.

It was Leroy. She knew it was he. He was down there in that dark stinking hole. She kept calling his name. The muffled grunts were coming nearer. Gradually she backed away but kept calling his name. She backed toward the hole in the floor, the grunts following her. She squirmed back up from under the floor and lay by the corpses, coaxing him out. "Come on, Leroy. Keep coming. Come home with Jasmin."

The top of his head broke out through the dark hole like a bright white flower—but there was old blood like rust on the white of his hair. Then he pushed his face up, his pale eyes blinking against the dim light.

Jasmin wanted to be sick.

Leroy's mouth was closed tightly on the body of a field mouse. Its tail hung down. Its funny stiff legs stuck out. Leroy was covered with brown filth and dried blood.

"Oh Leroy, love," Jasmin whispered in horror and tried to smile for him. He didn't stand up when he climbed out. He came toward her on all fours, using his knuckles like paws. He made noises more like an animal's than like a boy's as he went toward Jasmin, his mouth full of mouse, his eyes smiling in recognition, and sounds like purring coming from him.

Jasmin wanted to be sick but instead she leaned to meet him, firmly took the mouse from his mouth and set it carefully in a row with the others. She had to be careful not to upset him, not to send him into one of his fits.

She pulled up one of his filthy hands and persuaded him onto his feet. He smelled worse than any old bear. It was terrible to touch him but worse still to look at him. He looked like a bloodstained monster. Poor, poor Leroy. She had to get him home.

She helped him climb out into the sunshine and led him by the hand, with his pale eyes shut tight against the blinding sunlight.

The other kids screwed up their faces when they saw the mess Leroy was in, but not one of them said a word. On the long trek home Eglantine struggled with Carmen Miranda Elisa who was so heavy to carry. Nathaniel and Merron Damion Hugh forgot their bites and blisters and kept finding soothing leaves for Jasmin to hold on Leroy's eyes to cool them. It was a long, long way home.

But when they got there Olive didn't seem to see the terrible monster. She saw only Leroy, Leroy home safely. She hugged him in all his mess, and she stroked his bloodied hair. She told Eglantine to phone the police and everybody. That was just the right thing for Eglantine to do. She could enjoy feeling important.

For Olive to have all her children home again was happiness. She was her old smiling self, getting everybody organised.

"Nathaniel, bring in the bath."

"Merron Damion, can you stoke up the fire?"

"Jasmin, see to getting some water on the boil, love."

"Carmen, you go upstairs and find some clean clothes for Leroy."

"Marigold Lolita May, be a good girl and play with Honey Angelina while we all get Leroy clean."

All at once the Stalke house was a happy place again. They kneeled round the tin bathtub helping to soap Leroy who liked the nice warm water and all the loving attention. He made waves that splashed over onto the *for everything room* and no-body grumbled.

"Oh, will your Dad ever be a happy man when he gets home," Olive kept saying.

"And Jasmin, love, why don't you make some nice little chocolate cakes to celebrate when your Dad gets home and we're all together again."

33

THE NEXT DAY JASMIN WAS BACK IN SCHOOL. ALL the kids stared at her especially when the voice came over the intercom telling her to report to the principal's office. She stuck out her chin to pretend she didn't care. But she *did*. She guessed that everybody knew she'd tried to run away, even though the TV news had said she got lost. She felt pretty silly whatever anybody believed. It was awful being back in school. Girls stared at her, then whispered to each other.

Now Mr. Podluck, the principal, was keeping her waiting. Teachers' voices droned down the corridors. Little kids—still free—were shouting as they rode their tricycles down the street. Birds were wheeling, free. A train was being shunted down by the grain elevators. Jasmin imagined how it would be if she simply walked out of those doors, past the little kids, down to the elevators to the train. Where was the train going? East? West? Did it matter? She would like to hide in the train and be carried far away. But what about Leroy? Hadn't she caused him enough harm already?

Mr. Podluck kept her waiting for a very long time. She guessed she was going to get bawled out and have to listen to a long sermon. She could hear him on the phone talking about somebody who was too difficult to handle at home, somebody who needed special care and attention. Too much now for a family to cope with.

Jasmin moved from one leg to the other. Soon, she guessed, that voice would be telling her how good it would be for her to repeat grade six. She'd like to be rude and tell him that repeating grade six wouldn't make any difference to her. She felt very small and hopeless and angry and silly when at last he called, "You can come in now, Jasmin."

"Sit down," he said and pointed to a big shiny chair.

He sat on the edge of his table-desk and she kept her eyes down on his short white socks and the thin hairy bits of his legs that were showing.

"You've missed a lot of school," he said. As though she didn't know!

She just kept staring at his hairy shins.

"Your teachers say you don't show much interest in school, Jasmin. The guidance counselors have all said you could do much better if you tried harder."

She had heard it all before. She closed her mind, stopped listening, thought instead about her lovely hiding-hollow and the paint-smelling studio in the golden house. Oh, why did she have to be back here?

Then she heard Mr. Podluck saying magic-sounding words. "Jules Airlie, the naturalist, and Hana Townsend, the illustrator." She quickly looked up into Mr. Podluck's sharp, narrow eyes to hear what he was saying.

"Well, you seem to have made a good impression on them. Although they had to walk out because their road is still impassable and their vehicle stuck in the mud, they took the trouble to come all this way to talk to me. They think very highly of your abilities."

Before she could help it, her eyes filled with tears. That made her mad. She wasn't going to let Mr. Podluck see Jasmin Stalke cry. She stuck out her chin and stared at him, in spite of the silly tears that began to run down her silly face.

"So, Jasmin, your teachers and I have had a look at what work you have done. Your spelling's good. You express yourself well. I've talked to the principal at Witchitt—and we've decided to promote you into grade seven, to give you a chance to prove that you are capable, although your marks do not merit such a promotion. Here," he said gruffly and pushed a man-sized tissue at her. "Blow."

She didn't listen to the sermon he gave her. Instead she was sort of dancing inside and crying at the same time and her crazy mind was asking why everybody said THEM PEOPLE did terrible things.

"Yes, I know I shall have to work harder," she said at last. Then he let her go. She went into the girls' washroom to stare at herself in the mirror and to wait until nobody could tell she'd been crying before she went back to her class. She was glad she could say to her teacher's doubting question, "Yes, I do have a science project finished. My friends are going to deliver it to the arena." It was marvelous to be able to say she had an assignment done and even more marvelous to say, *"My friends."*

So, the first day back at school did have some good things in it and it wasn't so bad to face each day when she knew she was not going to be failed.

The day came when her class was taken on a school bus to set up their part of the science display. Some kids took their projects with them, some had their parents meet them at the arena bringing their experiments and equipment. Jasmin's project was there, as she knew it would be, on the long table reserved for the Dandron School display. Sheets of brown paper covered her work and each animal was wrapped in its private protection of cotton batting. The pine needles had been sprayed to keep them in place. The rivulet twinkled. Her hiding-hollow remained secret behind its skirting of spruce branches. She believed in it all again as she unwrapped her animals and arranged each one in its appropriate place. When she stood back to look, she could see that her project was nothing to be ashamed of. It was quite large among the Dandron projects.

As the Dandron kids were finishing up their displays, another school brought in its projects. Men and women all over the arena were covering long tables with white paper and setting up screens for displays of work. Jasmin looked around for Jules or Hana but didn't see them.

That afternoon, when the Stalke kids ran in from the schoolbus, there was a red Volkswagon by their door. A young man and woman were inside talking to Bud and Olive, but when the children came in they took time to tell them they were social workers who were there to discuss a few family problems. That was their job. Very interesting work, they said, because they got to meet so many interesting people.

Jasmin realized that this was what Mr. Podluck had been talking about on the phone when he kept her waiting so long outside his office. These social workers had come to suggest that Leroy go away. They explained there was a special home where he could get special attention and training. The idea made Olive cry but Bud said, "I guess the poor old boy has gotten too big for us to handle."

Jasmin felt terrible, that it was her fault Leroy was having to go away. She went over to him and held his strong hand in both hers, while she tried to concentrate on the idea that somewhere somebody could help him to find his mind and do useful things with his hands. Inside she knew that Leroy had to go away to get the help he needed. It was the way it had to be.

The social workers said, "He will be able to come home for holidays, once you get the upstairs made into separate rooms. He must have a room of his own."

Bud agreed cheerfully enough, rubbing his head and saying, "I guess it's time I divided that place up. I guess our kids are getting plenty big now."

"How time does fly," Olive sighed. "Seems no time since they was all babies, bless 'em."

The Stalke family waved as the red car drove

away. "We'll be in touch in a day or two," the lady called.

Then Jasmin went out to the pump with Leroy and silently cried as he pumped up the sparkling water. So many good things happening—but Leroy, Leroy.

34

Jasmin began to think her elementary school life was ending like a fairy story or a show on TV— well, almost.

She was going to get a private little room of her own. Her father was already putting up a framework for the walls and there were going to be two more windows in the attic. Eglantine was going to get one of them in her room.

And Jasmin Marie Antoinette Stalke was not going to fail.

After the long summer holiday Leroy would be going away to a school-home where specialists would help him, teach him things so one day he could earn a living and perhaps come home again.

But amazing, more amazing than anything, her mother and father were taking the whole family to the Witchitt Science and Art Fair. By Saturday all the judging was done and the Arena was open to the public.

"Come on, you kids," Bud, more cheerful these days, called to them. "Get yourselves cleaned up. Got to go to the show in Witchitt. They tell me our Jasmin has something worth looking at there."

They piled into the truck, Leroy and Honey Angelina in the cab with Bud and Olive, all the others ducking out of the wind in the back among bales of yellow straw. Jasmin had to hang onto the wild Marigold Lolita May to stop her from flying over the side.

When the Stalkes got there, the massive Witchitt Arena was crowded with people milling around. A high school band was playing marching music. The walls were bright with banners and pictures and signs and arrows. The aroma of hot dogs, onions and popcorn made mouths water. The Arena was like a market place, tables everywhere loaded with exhibits, big screens dividing the space up into little rooms where there were exhibitions of pictures, weavings, pottery, batiks—all sorts of things.

As soon as they got inside all the little Stalke kids wanted to get hot dogs but Olive said, "No. Oh, no, you don't. Not yet. Not till we've seen Jasmin's project."

Jasmin led them toward the Dandron table. It reminded her for a moment of her nightmare dream, but this time she wasn't carrying the cardboard box and Honey Angelina wasn't crying. "Look, it's over there." She pointed.

Just like her dream, her name had been written in spiky red handwriting, done with a thick Magic Marker. It said, *Jasmin Marie Antoinette Stalke,*

Dandron Elementary. She stopped dead still, with all her family around her.

"Look, Jasmin, at that big red thing over yours!"

"It shows you're a winner."

"Look, it says *second prize* in the middle of the red thing."

"Second *grand* prize."

"Nobody else from Dandron got a prize."

They were all talking at once. Olive held Honey Angelina in one arm and hugged Jasmin with the other, Jasmin who couldn't say anything. Her mouth seemed stuck open in a long unbelieving state of surprise. So, the judges *did* think it was a science project.

When they got up closer to the table, Bud said, "Eh, just look at them perfect little animals, will you." He touched each one with a thoughtful finger.

"They're real cute, Jasmin," Olive said and hugged Jasmin again.

Eglantine interrupted the scene by saying, "Let's go see what got first prize."

When they found the blue-ribbon rosette with *first prize* in the middle, way across the arena, they saw it belonged to somebody called Lazarus Zimmermann from Witchitt Elementary. Eglantine and Nathaniel began to giggle and say "What a crazy name." "Look at that name, will you!"

"Shhh," Jasmin nudged them both and whispered, "Shut up. He might hear."

Lazarus Zimmermann's exhibit looked very complicated with all sorts of charts and signs and fractions and calculations, all patiently and beautifully done and set out among magnifying lenses, reflectors, prisms and light bulbs. You could switch the lights on if you wished. Some people were switching the lights on and off while Nathaniel and Eglantine were still giggling. They kept mouthing "Lazarus Zimmermann" and bursting out into new fits of giggles. Jasmin kept saying "Shhh!" What if the boy were there and heard them.

"I don't care," said a voice next to her, and she turned to see a thin, scraggly boy with straight, lanky black hair and silver-rimmed spectacles. He looked very serious. "You're the girl," he said, and while he was saying it he put out his hand to shake hers. "I'm Lazarus Zimmermann," he said to Eglantine and Nathaniel as well as to Jasmin. He laughed too. "Guess some parents give kids funny names."

Jasmin was tongue-tied and felt foolish. No boy had ever shaken her hand before. It seemed to be a long handshake. There she was in the middle of the Witchitt Arena with people all around looking, and the winner of the *FIRST GRAND PRIZE*, a boy, was talking to her, the Stalke dummy kid.

He said, "Congratulations. You must be real clever to make things like that. I knew you were you because of your picture. You look exactly like your portrait down there."

Jasmin frowned. She had forgotten all about that in the excitement.

"Which picture's that?" Olive asked quickly.

"Haven't you seen it?" the lively Lazarus asked and pulled Jasmin by the hand while the rest of the family followed.

How could they possibly have missed it?

It was a big canvas, the biggest picture in the exhibition, larger than lifesize, of a girl walking proud as a queen in a beautiful flowing red gown, her eyes very blue and her thick straight hair lifting out behind her. In one hand she carried a broken straw hat like a big star against the gray stormy sky. Under the picture in simple printed black letters it said, "Jasmin Marie Antoinette Stalke by Hana Townsend."

How do you stop yourself crying when so many perfect things are happening, Jasmin wondered desperately. People were looking at her and she could feel her eyes filling with tears.

Doug Mason, the boy she had dreamed about who was always on the honor roll, walked right up to her and said, "Hi, Jasmin. You're not bad-looking, you know."

"Just like that portrait," said Lazarus. "I'd have recognised her anywhere."

Suddenly Leroy lifted both his big hands up toward the lovely portrait and cried out clear as clear, "Jasmin."

It was no good, even though she stuck out her chin, Jasmin Marie Antoinette Stalke had tears running down her cheeks for everyone to see. She couldn't stop crying. She was so happy.